Empty Quiver

War of the Submarine: Book 5.5

R.G. Roberts

Legacy Publishing LLC

Copyright © 2025 by R.G. Roberts

All rights reserved.

No part of this publication may be reproduced, distributed, or transmitted in any form or by any means, including photocopying, recording, or other electronic or mechanical methods, without the prior written permission of the publisher, except as permitted by U.S. copyright law. For permission requests, contact R.G. Roberts at www.rgrobertswriter.com.

The story, all names, characters, and incidents portrayed in this production are fictitious. No identification with actual persons (living or deceased), places, buildings, and products is intended or should be inferred.

No generative artificial intelligence (AI) was used in the writing or production of this work. All words, plots, and execution belong to the author. Without in any way limiting the author's exclusive rights under copyright, any use of this publication to "train" generative AI technologies to generate text is expressly prohibited. The author reserves all rights to license uses of this work for generative AI training and development of machine learning language models.

Cover designed by GetCovers.com

Edited by Jessica Meigs

This one is for Jess, my indefatigable editor who tore through *Rule the Waves* despite being as sick as a dog. Her enthusiasm and attention to detail continuously astound me. Any author can say that their editor is worth their weight in gold, but mine really is.

Contents

Epigraph	VI
1. Rogue Dragons	1
2. The Hard Choices	13
3. What Once Was Lost	24
4. The World Turned Upside Down	37
5. The Calm	44
6. Unlikely Friends	55
7. Operational Security	66
8. Compatriots	77
9. Ride the Storm	94
10. Epilogue: Still-Burning Embers	106
The Journey to Empty Quiver	118
Also by the Author	123
About R.G. Roberts	127

Epigraph

"The difference between a good and great officer is about ten seconds."

Admiral Arleigh Burke, USN

Chapter 1

Rogue Dragons

18 May 2040, The Andaman Sea

These had not been quiet waters since the opening days of the war.

The Andaman Sea sat between the Andaman Islands and Burma. North and west of it lay the Bay of Bengal, and south lay the Strait of Malacca, still the most contested waterway in the world. An average of two hundred ships transited the strait daily; that number was down from the war's beginning, when some days saw as many as four hundred ships travel through the SOM. Three battles for control of the waterway in the last two years, however, made some cargo-carrying companies nervous enough to send their ships the long way around, but going east and traveling through waters near Australia and New Zealand could add weeks to the journey.

Despite the danger, the bulk of the world's commerce still used the SOM. Like the Suez Canal, it was critical for goods moving to or from Europe and Asia, or Asia and the east coast of the Americas. Some intrepid companies shipping goods between the Americas and Asia chose to send their ships through the Pacific and then through the Panama Canal, but long wait times at the Panama Canal due to overloading caused the same sort of delays…and brought those ships back to the SOM.

With any merchant ship, time was money. The shorter a ship's master could make their journey, the more likely the crew was to get a bonus. In some cases, with refrigerated goods or other time-sensitive materials, extra time could ruin the cargo...which meant no quartet of merchant ships was likely to stop and loiter in the Andaman Sea. Not without good reason.

What their *good* reason consisted of, however, was hard to determine through sonar. Like any submarine, *Bluefish* used her ears as her eyes, listening through passive sonar to identify the "tracks," or surface and submerged ships and submarines around her. Listening to blade count, how fast a propellor turned, or even to the sounds of internal machinery let a submarine's sophisticated sonar suite identify what kind or class of ship they heard; good sonar operators—or systems, these days—could even identify individual ships. Chief Andreas, the *Bluefish's* chief sonar operator, had good reads on two of the four merchants; the other two weren't in the boat's sonar library, which meant they were probably new.

The other three contacts stopped in their vicinity, however, were what really got Alex's attention. Chief Andreas and her best protégée, Sonar Technician Submarines Second Class "Flo" Walkman, had identified one as a French frigate before she went all stop, but the other two had been lying in wait when *Bluefish* approached. Drifting—without putting power, and therefore noise, to their screws—was a surface ship's best tool for hiding from a submarine.

Surface ships that wanted to hide in the vicinity of another enemy warship were likely only one thing, but shooting without confirming that...

"Up scope," Captain Alex Coleman ordered as USS *Bluefish* (SSN 843) coasted up to periscope depth.

An early model *Cero*-class submarine, *Bluefish* fortunately lacked the always-up scope of her older *Virginia*-class sisters. Experience taught the U.S. Navy that the permanently extended periscope was convenient from a design perspective but damned *inconvenient* in both bad weather and emergency conditions; more than one *Virginia* had bent or broken a scope in the years since the class was first commissioned. Fortunately, the designers for the follow-on class listened to that lessons learned—though they ignored some others, much to the ire of Alex and other *Cero*-class captains—and brought back the old-school periscopes.

Bluefish's periscope slid up with the usual hydraulic whisper. The submarine maintained her course and speed at a mere three knots, which was barely enough to make way in the current sea state.

Today, Alex didn't press his face to the periscope eyepiece, despite his preference for the older technology. He'd grown up in *Virginia*-class boats, but his previous command, the late and great USS *Jimmy Carter*, had taught him to appreciate the feel of periscope handles under his hand and an eye on the target. But today he wanted a bigger picture, so he watched the periscope display screen over the tops of his reading glasses, hands in his pockets and head cocked.

Alex was an unassuming man; most people wouldn't look twice at him despite the silver eagles of a navy captain on the collar of his navy-blue coveralls. He was slim and kept his blond hair short; anyone who asked him would've been told his blue eyes were his best feature. Alex hated the fact he needed reading glasses as he approached forty, but there was no avoiding the fact that they reduced his headaches by a wide margin.

"What do you think, Bobby?" he asked his XO, or second-in-command.

Lieutenant Commander Robert O'Kane shrugged. His dark hair was a contrast to his captain, and he had several inches on him, too. Where Alex was unremarkable, Bobby had the kind of movie-star good looks that the navy would love to put on wartime recruiting posters. Part of Alex was surprised that Big Navy hadn't discovered that yet; unfortunately, they remained too obsessed with making *him* do interviews to notice his new XO.

Someday.

If he was lucky.

Bobby cleared his throat. "Well, I think that Weps wins the pool, sir. They're definitely boarding those poor suckers. Looks like Monsieur Frenchie wants to steal some stuff that's not his. Or hers."

Several people in *Bluefish's* control room snickered, making Alex grin. Every laugh or joke out of his crew—or the fact that his officers were willing to make bets concerning what the trio of French warships they were tracking was up to—marked a victory. Six months earlier, Alex had taken command of a submarine whose crew was broken and beaten down by bad leadership. Now they were an efficient team. Morale was high.

It helped that they'd taken out Captain Jules Rochambeau of the French attack submarine *Barracuda* less than a month earlier. *Bluefish*, once considered the worst boat in the U.S. Navy, had taken on the best in the world and won.

Now, after less than a week underway, they'd found more trouble.

Alex glanced at the screen again. All three gray-hulled ships were French frigates; from here—which was closer than was safe, a fact Alex had to admit to himself—they all looked like the same class. Squinting, he rolled through class characteristics in his mind until he landed on *Amiral Ronarc'h*. Yes, Chief Andreas was spot on yet again, wasn't she? She'd identified *Amiral Louzeau* right away, and she was the second ship of that class.

Well. This wasn't the best news. The *Amiral Ronarc'hs* were good at anti-submarine warfare. If Alex got stupid, they'd get him. Although the French hadn't built many of them, the ships were solid enemies. Even worse, two of their helicopters were already in the air. Those helos carried dipping sonar, one of the greatest threats to submarines.

The only question no one could answer from this distance was if the helicopters were already loaded out with torpedoes or depth charges. Right now, they appeared to be flying cover for the small boats zipping away from the frigates toward the merchant ships, so maybe they didn't have torps on board. Maybe they did. Alex didn't feel like finding out the hard way.

"Congratulations to Lieutenant Lange. You win the four-day special liberty chit." Alex grinned at his weapons officer, who just smirked.

"Thank you, sir," she replied. Some of the crew said Rose Lange *was* a weapon. Alex wasn't sure they were wrong.

No one doubted that Rose was a five-foot-six-inch, blond-haired firecracker whose focus put lasers to shame. She was tough, smart, and Alex knew she was going places. In fact, Rose was probably a better organized department head than Bobby had been; she was certainly more efficient. However, she was junior to him, and while Rose was a more driven manager, Bobby was a better all-around leader.

"All right, now that we know that the French want to keep these four British merchies, I think it's time to tell them we don't like that idea," Alex said. "Let's snap a few shots from the periscope camera for posterity and head back before we start firing."

"What, you don't want to pull a Convoy 57 and do it from here?" Bobby asked.

Alex turned a withering look on his XO. "You know I didn't actually shoot from periscope depth during that battle, don't you?"

"Uh. I'm guessing no, based on your reaction just now?" Bobby cringed. "Not my best question, was it?"

"Not even close." Alex sighed. He couldn't hold the verbal *faux pas* against his XO; Bobby was still way junior for the role. In fact, he'd only been boat's the official XO for a month and two days, and Bobby was still feeling his way into the job. Alex *had* requested him after Bobby filled in as acting XO on a temporary basis while the boat's navigator—and his predecessor cocked everything up by the numbers—but that didn't mean he shouldn't expect a few hiccups.

"You did go to periscope depth in the middle of an Indian formation and wait to be spotted, though, right?" Bobby asked. "I've heard a hundred stories about that. Pretty sure I read it in your patrol report, too."

"Sure I did." Alex shrugged. "But I was out of torpedoes by then. Think of it as a last-ditch, kind of insane, way to get them to pay attention to *Jimmy Carter* instead of the convoy. It worked, but they depth charged the shit out of us in exchange."

Bobby grimaced. "Ouch."

"You're telling me." Alex tried not to think on how it felt when he took his first boat to the bottom of the ocean floor...for the second time. Unlike most modern submarines, *Jimmy Carter* had been designed to bottom. However, it hadn't been gentle, and getting her off the ocean floor afterward took almost two hours. How maimed his submarine was after that, well, he didn't like thinking about outside his nightmares.

"I'd like to vote for not experiencing that," Rose said from the weapons corner.

"No shit." Alex grinned to chase away the demons. "*Bluefish* wouldn't take it nearly as well. Besides, the water's way too deep here."

The depth in the Andaman Sea varied wildly, but there were over eight thousand feet under *Bluefish's* keel at the moment. With a test depth of about fourteen hundred feet, Alex knew his crew would be pancakes long before the sub even saw the ocean floor.

Not a pretty thought.

Alex shook himself. His boat wouldn't go anywhere near the bottom if he kept his head in the game. "Officer of the Deck, submerge the ship. Make your depth three hundred feet."

"OOD, aye," Bobby replied. As the former navigator, who hadn't been replaced due to the navy's personnel system struggling to keep up with wartime demands, he continued to hold "the deck" at battle stations. Now he submerged the boat expertly, which Alex ignored.

"All right, folks, we're less than three nautical miles from these jokers," he said. "They haven't noticed us yet, but that's going to change in a hurry once we start shooting, and we don't have enough tubes to kill them all at once. So we're going to have to be cute about this."

"Do I want to know what you mean by cute?" Bobby asked.

Alex snorted. "Nope, but here we go. Weps, you have solutions on all three of our friends, yeah?"

"They're dialed in six ways 'till Sunday, sir," Rose replied.

"Good. We're going to have to split this up so we can keep them all busy, or one of them will try their best to kill us in the meantime," Alex said. "Odds are those helos will come for us with murder in their eye no matter what, but we can at least keep the frigates off our ass."

"There's some bugs on the windshield analogy here, but I can't find it." Bobby pouted.

"Beats a pop culture reference," Rose shot back.

Alex repressed a smile and glanced at the plot. "Weps, make all tubes ready in all respects, including opening the outer doors. Firing point procedures, tubes one and two, track 7879." That took care of the further contact, the one he could shoot at normally. Alex's standard procedure was to fire two torpedoes at any given target, then determine if another shot was needed. Unfortunately, he had three targets and only four torpedo tubes, and no matter how hard he tried, three times two just didn't come out to four. He took a deep breath.

"Make all tubes ready in all respects, including opening the outer doors; firing point procedures, tubes one and two, track 7879, Weps, aye."

"Firing point procedures, tube three, track 7880; tube four, track 7883."

Now math came to get him. Alex had two choices: shoot two torpedoes at one frigate and leave the other one until he could reload, or shoot one torpedo at each. The first choice gave him a higher hit probability, but it also meant the frigate who *hadn't* been shot at would be free to target *Bluefish*. Or the merchants. The only way to keep that French bastard busy was to shoot at him.

Rose repeated the order with no hesitation, and the fire control team did their usual quick job. Six months of mission after mission had turned *Bluefish's* crew into a well-oiled machine, and that was obvious when the boat was ready to shoot within moments.

"Solutions ready!" Rose said.

"Ship ready," Bobby added from her side.

"All tubes, fire."

Alex no longer felt the need to raise his voice. Why shout or even project a command when his crew knew their business? Control was quiet. No one needed him to show off, least of all the video data recorders high up on the bulkheads.

Four torpedoes raced out of *Bluefish's* tubes, heading for three oblivious French frigates. For them, today had been a quiet day with just another merchant ship boarding. Interdicting shipping in the Strait of Malacca was a strategic choice, and one that served their country well, but this was their second boarding of the day, and all three crews were bored. These four merchant ships would be inspected—because everyone lied about their cargo in these waters—and those not carrying goods critical to the war to enemies of the ULP would be allowed to proceed.

The plan for those aiding the enemy was to send them to the bottom. Unfortunately for the frigates, they never got to that part of the plan. *Amiral Louzeau* was the closest of the frigates, and unbeknownst to *Bluefish*, her onboard sonar was down for maintenance. Normally, she could depend on her sisters to extend their sonar envelopes to cover her; however, *Bluefish's* position shielded her from the other two frigates by sheer chance, *assuming* they would've been able to detect her in the first place. Regardless, in defiance of all modern technology, *Amiral Louzeau* never heard the single torp coming until it slammed right into her.

The torpedo hit *Amiral Louzeau* broadside, shooting a giant geyser of water into the air and breaking her keel. The French frigate's bow came up as her midsection sagged; then her stern rose out of the water as fires raged and sailors frantically abandoned ship. Within seconds, a modern, multi-million dollar frigate cracked in half and began sinking, taking most of her crew of almost one hundred and fifty with her.

Only then did her sisters start maneuvering. *Amiral Nomy*, the furthest of the three, dodged one of the torpedoes aimed at her, but the second one hit her stern-on, kicking her mangled aft end into the air with the force of the explosion. She sank more slowly but still followed suit. *Amiral Castex*, the middle frigate, made the mistake of turning away from *Amiral*

Louzeau and into the path of a torpedo meant for her sister, *Amiral Nomy*. While dodging that one, she put herself right back into the path of the torpedo *Bluefish* aimed at her, which took her bow off and left her sinking by the head.

Alex returned to periscope depth, shot some more photographs for posterity, and made sure the boarding teams had left the merchant ships before departing. That took a few creative threats, but he found that the presence of *Bluefish* was an effective scare tactic, and the French boarding teams evacuated to their boats with a bit of coaxing.

"Well, that's that," Bobby said as *Bluefish* slipped back beneath the waves. "What's next, Captain?"

"Eager for more action, already?" Alex laughed. "What kind of monsters have I created here?"

Pride made him feel lightheaded. If his crew had become monsters, it was indeed Alex's doing. Six months ago, *Bluefish* had been the dregs of the barrel. The worst of the worst. What was it that Uncle Marco told him? *She hasn't exactly covered herself in glory so far. I want you to change that.* Alex shivered. Heaven help him, he'd done that. Now his crew was confident, bold, and even a little cocky. Just the way Alex liked them.

"Well, Uncle Marco loves to give us the hard jobs, so it figures that he's got something else in the queue," Bobby replied.

Uncle Marco was the king of submarines in the Indian and Pacific Oceans, otherwise known as Commander, Submarine Forces Pacific, or COMSUBPAC. Foul-mouthed, blunt, and charismatic, Admiral Marco Rodriquez was popular with the entire sub force, both for his down-to-earth style and practical leadership. After a rocky start to the war where one out of every three American submarines deployed never came home, Uncle Marco made sure every boat was properly manned, equipped, and ready to fight.

He gave them what was needed, but he also asked for a lot. Like now.

Alex's smile turned crooked. "We're in for an interesting ride. There are rumors of a secret base of some sort near New Caledonia, so guess where we're off to?"

"That's on the entire opposite coast of Australia," Rose said.

"Right in one. So we'll slip down the SOM, go through the—"

A voice from the intercom, or bitch box, next to Alex cut in before he could finish describing their next audacious mission. "Captain, Radio, flash traffic from COMSUBPAC. It's..."

The radio watch trailed off, suddenly silent. Faint sounds of movement came over the internal net, followed by a *thunk*, and then the line died. A moment later, Ensign Charlie Maguire stumbled into control, his freckled face pale. Maguire was *Bluefish's* communications officer, and he'd been on board a few months longer than Alex. That meant he was too experienced to fall out of the radio room with wide eyes and a punch-drunk expression.

"What's the flash traffic, Commo?" Alex asked.

Maguire swallowed. "It's an Empty Quiver, sir. Someone stole a Chinese boomer armed with twelve JL-3 SLBMs."

"What?" Alex's jaw dropped.

His hand wanted to shake as Alex accepted the message tablet. He'd never *dreamed* of receiving an Empty Quiver message outside of drills. Hell, Alex couldn't remember the last time the navy even *practiced* what to do in the event of a nuclear weapon—or a boat full of them—being stolen. The very idea left him cold.

Skimming the message, Alex felt rooted to the spot with shock and no small amount of fear. This war—the first world war in almost a century, in a world which had believed itself past such things—had defied "expert" opinions by not going nuclear. But why would any developed nation want to reach for the ultimate tool of Armageddon? Even a first strike guaranteed destruction; too many nations were armed with nuclear weapons, and *someone* would strike back. A nuclear war had no winners. Not with the potential of a fallout-caused nuclear winter or electromagnetic pulses destroying critical infrastructure. The world would lose. Everyone knew that.

Every *nation* knew that. What about this so-called Undersea Liberation Army? Alex swallowed.

FLAGWORD/NAVY BLUE/EMPTY QUIVER//

TIMELOC/180643MAY2040/NORFOLK/INIT//

GENTEXT/

1. INCIDENT: CHINESE JIN-CLASS BALLISTIC MISSILE SUBMARINE STOLEN BY UNKNOWN FORCES

2. DATE OF INCIDENT: 02 MAY 2040

3. TIME OF INCIDENT: UNKNOWN, LATE AFTERNOON

4. LOCATION OF INCIDENT: JIANGGEZHUANG, CHINA, SUBMARINE BASE NO 1

5. INCIDENT: UNKNOWN FORCES, POSSIBLY ASSOCIATED WITH A TERRORIST GROUP, INVADED THE DEMOCRATIC REPUBLIC OF CHINA BASE IN JIANGGEZHUANG. A SHORT BATTLE ENSUED BEFORE THREE (3) SUBMARINES GOT UNDERWAY WITHOUT CLEARANCE FROM LOCAL AUTHORITIES. THESE THREE UNITS CONSIST OF:

(1) JIN-CLASS TYPE 094 SUBMARINE CARRYING UP TO TWELVE (12) JL-3 SUBMARINE LAUNCHED BALLISTIC MISSILES. PRC DESIGNATION WAS CHANGZHENG 14.

(2) SHANG-CLASS TYPE 093 ATTACK SUBMARINES.

TAIWANESE FORCES SANK ONE ATTACK SUBMARINE. REMAINING ATTACK SUBMARINE IS CHANGZHENG 18, TYPE 093A. SURVIVORS FROM SUNKEN CHANGZHENG 9 CLAIMED TO BE FROM THE UNDERWATER LIBERATION ARMY, A HERETOFORE UNKNOWN TERRORIST OR FREEDOM-FIGHTING ORGANIZATION.

6. DAMAGE: UNKNOWN DAMAGE TO SUBMARINE BASE NO 1. TAIWANESE INTELLIGENCE INDICATES THAT THE UNDERSEA LIBERATION ARMY IS NOT ALLIED WITH TAIWAN OR THE DEMOCRATIC REPUBLIC OF CHINA.

7. UPDATES TO FOLLOW. ALL UNITED STATES SUBMARINES TO BE AWARE OF POTENTIAL HOSTILE ACTION FROM CHANGZHENG 14 AND CHANGZHENG 18./

Chapter 2

The Hard Choices

Approaching Anniversary Escape Station (Independent)

"This place was a dump *before* the attack. I hate to see what it looks like up close, now," STS1 Nathan "Bud" Wilson muttered, gesturing at the outline of an underwater station on the tactical screen on the top of his console.

The sonar supervisor console on USS *Kansas* (SSN 810) consisted of three vertically stacked monitors. The top was a tactical fusion plot, where fire control, navigation, and sonar data supposedly all came together to provide operators with a real-time picture of their operating environment. The middle was the traditional waterfall screen, where purists like Wilson could look at the raw data. The bottom was both the computer interface and additional raw sonar data, including direct control over the *Virginia*-class submarine's passive and active sonar arrays.

"You been there?" STS2 Mary Zins asked. In her short time on *Kansas*, Zins had quickly become Wilson's number two sonar operator, and not only because she was the next most senior person on a boat that didn't have a chief, but also because she was *smart*.

Wilson liked smart. Being too smart was a problem he liked to have...even when his superiors disagreed with it.

"Yeah. Couple years back, *Bluefish* pulled in there because we had something broken. I can't remember what. Something new was always broken on that boat. Or the bow thruster. That was just always broken." He didn't add that it was never something critical, not with Commander Peterson. Grandma Peterson was a pro at finding any reason to avoid a fight, and pulling into Anniversary Escape had been yet another time Peterson skated out of doing his duty.

"So why's it a dump?" Zins kept her voice down. *Kansas* was at battle stations, and the captain and XO were busy conferring in the corner, but everyone knew that Lieutenant Commander Song disapproved of casual chit-chat.

As if talking to each *other* would stop them from shooting bad guys. Wilson barely managed not to roll his eyes, but he *did* stop himself. He was redeemed these days, wasn't he?

"I mean, it's a tourist trap, or was, I guess, but it looks like it was built in the 1980s. My parents stayed somewhere classier on their honeymoon, and they're old as fucking dirt." He grinned. "Supposedly, there's a gold mine somewhere under the place, but if there is, they're sure as shit spending that money on something other than making Anniversary Escape look like a place people want to escape to."

Zins snickered. "I'll cross it off my bucket list, then."

"Good idea, since its TRANSPLATs are on fire."

"Are you two *finished*?" Inevitably, Song stalked over to ruin the fun.

Zins flinched; Wilson just gave the XO his best smile.

"Standing by for orders, XO," he said. "We're still tracking Mister Mystery Contact over there by the station. He's still hidden in the churn of the small boats in the water and whatever the hell exploded or imploded before we got here. No way to tell what he is."

"Hm." Song shot him a narrow-eyed glare that did nothing to make her look less mean.

Wilson shrugged. "Can't identify what I can't hear, ma'am."

"Of course you can't," the XO snapped before turning away.

Commander Kennedy, the boat's XO, approached. Unlike the XO, he looked thoughtful, with his head cocked and gaze distant. But Wilson knew that was a ruse. Kennedy's temper was like a lit firecracker, always ready to explode. However, sometimes he liked to play the reasonable and measured captain. Was this one of those moments, or would Kennedy get bored and order *Kansas* to go haring off to patrol areas outside the scope of their orders yet again?

Wilson decided to take a chance.

"You want to go to periscope depth and identify this guy, sir?" he asked.

Kennedy pursed his lips. "Perhaps." He glanced at Song. "What do you think, XO? You want to take a look around?"

"It might be more efficient than waiting to hear something." Song didn't quite glare at Wilson, but the message was loud all the same.

He let Zins do the sweep when ordered so the boat rose toward the surface. Surfacing, or even coming to periscope depth, was an evolution that took forever and a day during peacetime, but war cut a few steps—and safeties—out of the evolution. No surprise there. Everything had to be faster when people might start shooting; the U.S. Navy had learned that the hard way. Stealth might mean life, but speed was the best way to avoid death.

Wilson just concentrated on trying to figure out what the hell that contact dancing around behind Anniversary Escape's two TRANSPLATs, or TRANSportation PLATforms, was. He didn't usually have trouble classifying surface contacts, but this dude was clever, keeping the noise of the burning platform to the east and the boats zipping around in the water between himself and *Kansas*. Wilson frowned. Did he know a sub was tracking him?

What kind of ballsy motherfucker hung around when an American submarine wanted to put a torpedo in him?

"What *is* that?" Song asked, her voice quiet and curious.

"That's a goddamned *Yantar*," Kennedy hissed. "That's a fucking Russian intelligence trawler pulling survivors out of the water."

"That's not a Russian station," Weps said from the fire control corner.

"Thank you for pointing out the obvious, Weps." Kennedy twisted to stare at his favorite department head.

"I mean, are they there to help? Maybe there was an accident instead of an attack?" Weps asked.

"Fuck." Kennedy scowled. "If they didn't do this..."

"Then we will face scrutiny if we torpedo a ship engaged in search and rescue," Song said.

"God*damn* it!" Kennedy slapped the navigation table, his flat palm making a *cracking* noise that caused several watchstanders to jump. Not Wilson; he'd expected some sort of bullshit. There always was on this boat. "Just when we find a good target, the fucking Russian has to go and *help* people!"

"We could warn them off, maybe?" Lieutenant Sue Grippo, the navigator, said.

Kennedy twisted to glare at her. "Don't be more stupid than God made you, Nav. They'd still have survivors on board, and then *we'd* look like the assholes if we shot them while people suffered." He gestured at the periscope view screen, where the burning TRANSPLAT was visible...as were people in the water. "Attack submarines are shit for search and rescue. We can't pick them up."

"More importantly, we don't know which ones of them would be enemies." Song's nose twitched. "Particularly on a so-called independent station."

Now Wilson finally let himself roll his eyes, but he was smart enough to face his console before he did it. What horseshit. Anniversary Escape might not owe allegiance to Australia, but its owners knew which side its bread was buttered on. That prissy-ass place was located between Saladin Underwater Research Station, which was owned by the Australian government, and Peter Point, which was owned by a major Australian conglomerate. Eighty-plus percent of its yearly visitors were Australian. Another ten percent were New Zealanders.

Unless the owners were flaming morons, they weren't going to cozy up to the Russians of all people. Certainly not in the middle of a war where Russia owned *zero* assets in the Indian

Ocean. Sure, they'd done a bang-up job of stealing stations and islands from the Japanese, but the northern Pacific was a long way from here.

"You're right, of course." Kennedy crossed his arms. "I suppose that fucker gets away this time."

"Excuse me, Captain." Chief Brown appeared, as if by magic, and Wilson twisted in surprise. Brown and his radio heads got their own little space hidden away from the rest of the watchstanders in control, a fact that left Wilson unaccountably jealous. Every other class of submarine had a sonar room, but no, not the *Virginias*. Even the Block V boats like *Kansas* hadn't fixed that stupid design mistake, but they still let the radio weenies hide!

"This had better be good, Chief." Kennedy turned his glare on Brown, who just extended one of the boat's message tablets.

"OPREP-3 Empty Quiver message, sir," Brown said, his normally booming voice flat. "It's real. Looks like some terrorist group has stolen a Chinese boomer."

Wilson froze.

Kennedy stared, pale-faced, for a long moment before snatching the tablet and reading the message. Then his face grew red.

"You've got to be *shitting* me," he snarled.

"What's wrong?" Song asked.

"They've sent *Bluefish* after the Chinese terrorists. Of fucking course they have." Kennedy looked down at the tablet once more before flinging it into a nearby bulkhead. It hit hard, bouncing off an angle iron, and then landed on the deck with that *pancake* noise that told Wilson the screen was shattered.

Sure enough, once Brown picked it up, he was proven right. Even military-grade technology couldn't stand up to temperamental captains, could it?

"Get me all the information we have on these fuckers," Kennedy said. "I want to find them first."

The Seychelles

Captain First Rank Katerina Revnik despised this tropical island. Oh, the Seychelles were nice—if one liked beaches—but there wasn't much to do aside from sunbathe or casino hop, neither of which interested her much. Her nation's French allies spoke endlessly of this place, calling it paradise and waxing poetic about how the Seychelles rejoining with France promised a new age of French prosperity, but Katerina knew that for what it was: utter bullshit. The Seychelles were allied with the Union for the Liberty and Prosperity of the Indian Ocean (ULP), yes, but they remained an independent nation. Any Frenchman who thought otherwise was delusional.

Besides, she preferred the ambiance and the islands of the Mediterranean. The weather was nicer, too, even if her crew loved the casinos here. Sailors were sailors, she supposed. But Katerina had other interests.

Despite a long history of wars and naval conflict, the Mediterranean Sea was an odd sort of middle ground in World War III, sort of like a neutral bubble where the belligerents were *almost* civil with one another. Why? No one really knew, aside from the presence of other, non-aligned powers who were not prepared to put up with violence from either the ULP or the Grand Alliance. Spain, Italy, and Egypt led resistance against any belligerent actions. The European Union officially condemned France's warmongering and had threatened to eject the nation no less than five times, but so far the EU remained intact and the best bulwark against a full war in the Mediterranean.

Katerina was grateful for that. The best ports to visit were all in the Mediterranean Sea, and most of those were *not* French.

She was particularly fond of Greece, and so long as her nation promised not to attack Greek or other EU shipping, her beautiful new submarine was welcome there. In fact, *Andromeda* had just finished a lovely five-day visit to Rhodes before they were summoned to the Seychelles for the final training portion of their shakedown cruise, and the week-long voyage from Greece to the Indian Ocean did nothing to cure her cravings for the Greek Island's food, history, and tranquility.

Unfortunately, her current companion was anything but tranquil. Katerina kept her face neutral as she watched Camille Dubois through narrowed eyes; the Frenchwoman was both beautiful and dangerous, but there was a darkness lurking behind those traits that made Katerina wary. Dubois's competence was well-established, as was her status as Jules Rochambeau's tactical protégée...but Katerina was not overly concerned about that. Rochambeau had propositioned her the one time they met, and like her, he'd lost his submarine to Alex Coleman.

Unlike Katerina, Rochambeau was now rotting in an American POW camp. She resisted a smile. Who was more successful now? Records were not everything. She had time.

"I will need three days to get underway." Dubois's face grew pinched. "And the contractors still working on my combat systems suite *must* finish their work by tomorrow. Then *Perle* will be able to respond to this threat."

Katerina finally let her nose curl. "I do not think we have three days," she said, folding her hands in her lap.

Now was the time to portray the good ally, the conscientious officer. Katerina was among allies but not friends; aside from her, there was one Russian liaison officer in this sea of French faces. She was her nation's representative, and she had to be perfect. Every eye upon her would judge Russia by her actions. It helped that she was also pretty, with a figure-skater's form and a heart-shaped face that made men stupid. Her dark hair was contained in an elegant braid, and her uniform was always perfect, because Katerina knew that the Russian navy *needed* its stars and she had been chosen to be one.

Her superiors had been very clear on that when they gave her *Andromeda*. She was needed. Time and communism had all but destroyed the proud Russian navy; the force that rose from its ashes was still finding itself. Oh, they were fierce and they were many—Russia had never had a problem manning ships, only with building ones good enough to help sailors in the fight—but sometimes, they felt rudderless. Even two years into the war, Katerina remained familiar with that feeling of drift and confusion. Rebuilding a navy's soul was hard.

Dubois twisted to face her. "Then what *do* you suggest?"

"*Andromeda* will go after this threat." Katerina kept her voice level. "We are ready. Time is of the essence. The decision is simple."

Admiral Fournier, an extremely tall man with a silver unibrow and crooked nose, scowled. "This should be a joint operation."

"I only speak of what is possible." Katerina shrugged. "Work a miracle and get *Perle* ready, and I will be happy to cooperate with Russia's allies."

Fournier glared. "Of course you would."

"Admiral, I am not trying—" Katerina cut off as Fournier's aide stepped forward to whisper in his ear. She stared, not expecting the sheer rudeness. She and Dubois were both full captains, and Fournier was a two-star admiral. What small-minded junior officer thought he could interrupt this critical conversation? She felt her spine stiffen. "Is there a problem, Lieutenant?"

The French lieutenant glanced her way, lifting her nose like Katerina was a bad Russian smell. She did not answer, but Fournier looked up from the tablet she had handed him, his face solemn.

"Our governments are meeting at an emergency meeting of the United Nations," he said.

Dubois snorted. "The U.N. is a paper tiger."

"Obviously." Fournier sneered. "But the leadership of both the ULP and the Grand Alliance has agreed to meet."

"They have?" Katerina sat up straight, her heart pounding.

From where she was sitting, it felt like the world had tripped into war. While France and India had hungered for additional territory, and they thought they could get away with grabbing Armistice Station, the largest underwater station in the world. Armistice Station's independence meant they might've gotten away with it...had circumstance not led a trigger-happy American admiral to accidentally fire on an Indian *Kilo*-class submarine in the Strait of Malacca. The resulting all-out carrier battle was the harbinger of war.

Like any loyal Russian, Katerina did not mind. Her country needed the prestige, power, and influence that came with war. Not to mention resources and territory. Stung by events in the first quarter of the twenty-first century, Russia grew wise and waited for another nation to start a war before leaping into the fray. That way, others took the blame...and Russia seized what she needed. And what had Russia accomplished so far? On the surface, it might appear to be less than the French gains of territory and underwater stations in the Indian and Pacific Oceans, or the Indian territory in Pakistan. Yet many of those gains were likely temporary. Whatever treaty ended the war would force the Indians and French to give much of that territory—and those critical, *rich* stations—back.

Neither Katerina nor her countrymen were under any illusions. This war would someday end, likely in a negotiated settlement. When that day came, France and India would be forced to answer for their boldness. But Russia? Russia joined her allies on principle, and the territory she had quietly acquired was in already disputed waters. Yes, the Japanese claimed the waters where the twenty-six—no, twenty-nine as of yesterday—stations were located. However, Russia's historic claims to those waters were equally strong. Any postwar peace would recognize that.

Yes, Russia had also secured several formerly independent stations in the Baltic Sea, but none were individually rich enough to gain backing from the Grand Alliance. Nor were the three in the North Sea, save the one sprawling British station located midway between Denmark and the United Kingdom. In a perfect world, Russia might nip out and take pieces of

Finland, but every Russian knew that land conquest was a bad idea. Those lessons were written in blood. Territory with *history* would have to be returned. This was not the 1900s. People did not forgive.

"*Casse-toi.*" Dubois rolled her eyes. Katerina, who spoke English—the language of this meeting—but not French, chose not to ask for a translation. The dismissive tone said enough.

"What are they meeting about?" Her heart pounded; Russia could not afford peace *now*, could they?

Katerina turned the idea over in her head. Perhaps if the world hated India and France more, Russia might slip through the cracks and keep her prizes. The recent and publicized capture of Jules Rochambeau meant the French were on enemy minds. Was it possible?

"They speak of an armistice." Admiral Fournier licked his lips. "Temporarily."

"What can we gain if they stop shooting?" Now Dubois sat up straight, her blue eyes intent. Damn the woman. Katerina didn't want to dislike an ally even more than she had the obnoxiously flirtatious captain Dubois once served under, but the hungry and cold glint in Dubois's eyes made Katerina twitchy.

No. She should not fantasize about sinking allies.

"What will the armistice mean?" Katerina asked to bring the meeting back on track.

"That is yet to be determined," Fournier replied.

He did not tell Dubois not to violate those potential agreements with their current enemies, Katerina noted. Nor did he seem optimistic about peace. *Temporary*, he'd said. Yes, it made sense. No one with sense wanted some rogue group sailing the seas with a ballistic missile submarine. Civilized nations would not tolerate a wild card like that. This Undersea Liberation Army had to be stopped.

"Then I will get underway, regardless." Katerina rose. "My respects to you and your crew," she added with a nod to Dubois, "but armistice or not, we still must deal with the threat at hand, no?"

Dubois made a face. "Obviously."

"Then *Andromeda* will set out to find these stolen Chinese submarines," she replied. "I will await word from my government before taking action against anyone else."

She caught Captain Third Rank Lebedev's eye. Lebedev was naval intelligence, but he understood submarines better than most of his ilk. His crisp nod promised he'd get word to her, so Katerina left without looking back. Fournier was not her commanding officer. She owed him nothing beyond the respect due an ally.

This was her moment. If she could find and destroy that stolen ballistic missile submarine, *Katerina* would be the submariner whose name was on everyone's lips. The world would forget Jules Rochambeau and Alex Coleman. Russian skill and sea power would be on display for the world to see. And Katerina would finally rise.

All she had to do was find the damned thing.

Chapter 3

What Once Was Lost

ARMISTICE DECLARED: WARRING NATIONS UNITE TO FIND STOLEN NUCLEAR MISSILE SUBMARINE
Mark Easley, *The Washington Post*
MAY 19^(TH)—*The Hague.* History was made today...for however long it lasts. Yesterday, Taiwanese intelligence leaked information to both American and Indian governments that a previously unknown terrorist group known as the Undersea Liberation Army had stolen three Chinese nuclear submarines. One of these submarines, a *Shang*-class attack submarine, was immediately sunk by the Taiwanese Navy. However, the other two—another *Shang*- and a *Jin*-class ballistic missile submarine—escaped.

The last year of war has taught the public to be cautious. Perhaps it has even taught fear. But the one thing we have all been confident in, perhaps too confident in, was our nations' promises that they would not turn to nuclear weapons. War may be terrible, but mutually assured destruction is beyond the pale. No nation wants to destroy the world, no matter what their territorial ambitions are. So a lucky thirteen months of war has bought us death and bloodshed on the high seas, but no nuclear weapons.

We had grown confident in that. Comfortable. Until now. Now there is a *Jin* on the loose. That submarine sports a dozen ballistic missiles, and each of *those* carries multiple reentry vehicles. Does the Undersea Liberation Army have the launch codes? The Taiwanese don't think so, but the world is holding its breath.

And so fear breeds peace. In a shocking move, representatives of both the Grand Alliance and the Union for the Liberty and Prosperity of the Indian Ocean met at the Hague late yesterday. In a closed-door meeting that lasted well into the night, those representatives hashed out a genuine armistice—a ceasefire—that will last at least until the stolen submarines are found. If the world is fortunate, we will find common ground during this emergency and stop the war entirely. All military actions will cease as of midnight GMT tonight. Any commanders or units breaking that prohibition will be prosecuted to the full extent of their nation's laws. (Read the full text of the armistice on the *Post* website here.)

Now the world holds its breath.

Now the race is on to find the stolen missile submarine. Rumor already says that the best submarine hunters across six navies have been sent to scour the waters near China. Diplomatic protests from two of three Chinese governments have already been lodged—two were present at the Hague; Taiwan voted in favor of both the armistice and the combined effort to find the rogue submarines—but the immediate concern is finding the *Jin* before anyone is killed. Or before nuclear war ruins the world.

The *Post* will be covering the search as well as publishing a series of articles taking an in-depth look at the loss of both submarines in the coming days.

Commander, Submarine Forces Pacific Headquarters, Pearl Harbor, Hawaii

Vice Admiral Winifred Hamilton sighed and put the tablet down. Reading the article for a second time only made her headache pound harder. "This Easley fellow has a way with words, doesn't he?"

"He's better than the fucking idiot fearmongers who are telling people it's time to dig a basement or a grave, their pick." Vice Admiral Marco Rodriquez, the owner of the posh but mostly empty office they sat in, didn't even look up from the computer mouse he was disassembling. "Neither would save them from a goddamned nuclear holocaust, but what the fuck do I know?"

"The navy *did* send us to nuclear power school. Not how-to-build-a-missile school." Freddie eyed the mouse and decided it was a lost cause. Maybe she should buy him something indestructible for his upcoming birthday.

Knowing Marco, he'd find a way to take the thing apart, anyway.

Freddie sighed. She'd known Marco Rodriquez since they were both young division officers, still learning the ways of submarine life. He'd been her friend when others mocked and derided her, trying to force "a girl" out of submarines. The joke was on them now; all of her detractors had resigned or retired, and Freddie Hamilton was Commander, Submarine Forces: owner of all American submarines.

She was also her best friend's boss, which made things awkward at times like this. Never had they imagined winding up in a situation like this, where Freddie was a hair senior to Marco, yet they *also* had to work as a team, because her other job of Commander, Submarine Forces Atlantic meant she was in direct control of all Atlantic Ocean–based squadrons. The bulk of the war remained in Marco's front yard, which meant Freddie's boats crossed over and became Marco's. It might've made for an epic tug of war had they worked together less well, but fortunately, the admirals understood that open communication was key to victory.

An onlooker could've been excused for wondering why they were friends. They were physical opposites, with Freddie tall, pale, dark-haired, and serious suffering in comparison to Marco's short, Hispanic, "dirty troll" persona. He swore up a storm, drank like a fish, and seemed to command off instinct alone; she liked quiet evenings with her cats, briefed the CNO with stacks of facts, and had once been accused of studying a problem to death. But Freddie wasn't afraid of a fight any more than Marco was afraid of a good spreadsheet; they were both sharp, focused, and determined to overcome the multitude of ways in which their predecessors failed the sub force.

"Eh. I figured that part out when I was stationed on a boomer." Marco shrugged.

"You would." Freddie had commanded a boomer, USS *Columbia*, but she'd always been horrified at the idea of firing her missiles. Yes, she'd resigned herself to following orders someday if she had to, but she was very glad she'd never had to turn that firing key.

Marco grinned. "Yeah."

"All right, what's the play, COMSUBPAC?" she asked, keeping her voice light. "We have targets, and the subs nearby are yours. I'm not here to micromanage you. Who do you want to send?"

"You might be the only admiral in fucking history who goes *toward* the nuclear threat instead of running away," he replied. "Speaking of idiots. Sane people run from nuclear destruction. But anyway, if you want to burn with me, who the fuck am I do argue? *Bluefish* is the sub. Coleman's the man. He just sank Rochambeau when no one else could. This shouldn't be beyond him."

Freddie bit her lip to stop a snarl from escaping. Of course Marco would pick Captain Alex Coleman. Under other circumstances, she would've said that Marco chose Coleman just to annoy her, because he *knew* that Freddie had a colorful history with the man. She didn't approve of Coleman's habit of living outside the box; she wasn't sure the man knew that the box existed, let alone where it was. Freddie scowled. No. That was wrong. Coleman knew damned well where the box was. He just chose to ignore it.

Yet there was no denying the man's success rate. He'd gone from relative but annoying unknown to the sub force's star in just six months. From having smashed every record defending Convoy 57—whilst winning the Medal of Honor—to taking

Bluefish out of the dumpster and making the boat the go-to submarine for America's hardest tasks, it was hard to argue Alex Coleman wasn't *able* to do this task. In fact, his innovative nature might line him right up for finding a submarine driven by motivated amateurs who might do anything. Still, Freddie was left uncomfortable every time she thought back on their harrowing escape from Armistice Station on the eve of the war. Coleman's genius saved them, yet the man was so damned...insolent. No. Cocky? Perhaps audacious was the right word.

Whatever the man was, he was a menace.

"I know you don't fucking like him," Marco said before Freddie crawled out of her thoughts. "But *Bluefish* is already underway, and you can't knock his record. Everything he touches turns to goddamned gold."

"Or hits the bottom, yes." Freddie was polite enough not to mention that Coleman sent his *last* boat to the bottom, too. *Jimmy Carter* had just been tough enough that the bastard was able to pick her up again and get back into the fight. She sighed. "Your point is made. Send him."

Marco flashed her a grin. "Send him, aye."

Freddie didn't watch or listen as he shouted for his aide and the two worked out the official orders; it was Marco, and any administrative work he did would undoubtedly be the bare minimum. But his leadership and organizational talent far outweighed his hatred of paperwork; Marco wasn't the first man promoted to COMSUBPAC during this war, but he'd already lasted longer than his predecessor. He was also far better at the job.

Only Marco Rodriquez could hold the deployments and missions of over thirty submarines *in his head* and never miss a beat. He had a status board on the far wall that showed the location of every PACFLT submarine...but Freddie had never once seen him consult it.

She busied herself checking her email. Being away from the East Coast for so long was risky; Freddie knew something would go wrong while she was gone. It almost had to. Murphy's Law was alive and kicking harder than ever with the war on. Whether it would be more sunken boats, construction delays, or weapons issues, she didn't know, but the next albatross was sure to be lurking around the corner.

A new message popped up, and Freddie skimmed it before glancing up at Marco. "You want to send a second boat?" she asked. "*Kansas* is underway and in the vicinity of Christmas Island."

"You've seen how Kennedy and Coleman get along, haven't you?" Marco arched an eyebrow. "They make me and Rick Thorton look like best fucking friends."

Freddie winced, remembering a fist fight back at the sub school. Marco, scrappy bastard that he was, won, but both he and Thorton suffered for it. They'd been lucky not to get kicked out. "Yes, I'm aware of their mutual affection," she replied.

Marco hooted in laughter. "Right, you took Coleman to mast on Kennedy's recommendation."

"Unfortunately."

"Well, then, don't stick them together for a mission. It'd be combustive, and Coleman's reflexes are quicker." Marco cocked his head. "Fucker's smarter, too. Though probably not as ruthless."

"I cannot argue with that assessment, although I'll point out that a certain degree of ruthlessness is necessary in this game."

"The one you and I have never played?" He snorted. "Don't put too many cooks in the kitchen. Kennedy will get in the fucking way. Just let Coleman work his magic."

Her eyes narrowed. "This is hardly a situation where we can afford failure. Or even delay."

"All right. Sure. Fine. Send *Kansas* up through the SOM. That'll tell us if the armistice is *really* going to hold, as the ULP has an epic hard on for the Strait of Malacca. That should block the not-Chinese subs from escaping, too. Then he can mosey on up to the South China Sea and start searching there."

"Intelligence says the contacts are still in the *East* China Sea."

"Yeah, but submarines move. This lets us be there if they move southwest. You're right that *Kansas* is best positioned for that. She'll be our blocker. If she gets there in time, she'll be the one who stops them. Assuming they get through *Bluefish*."

He had to add that last sentence, didn't he? Freddie didn't bother groaning. She knew Marco far too well to chastise him. He wouldn't learn.

"I'll send the orders," she said instead. "Let's find these assholes so we can sleep in peace."

"No shit," Marco said with feeling.

20 May 2040, The South China Sea

Changzheng 7 was on the hunt. Although their chain of command remained unclear, with three different Chinese governments desiring command over the *Shang*-class boat, all parties agreed on two things: the two stolen submarines had to be found, and it was best if a Chinese submarine did so.

Commander Liao Fan didn't know how many other Chinese boats from the three competing Chinas were underway. He just knew that "*Seven*," as *Changzheng 7* was known, was short on sailors, food, and weapons. They'd been fortunate to have enough crew on board to get underway, but keeping her that way was hard. Nuclear attack submarines were built to be underway for months at a time, but for a submarine that had not submerged in over two years, eighteen days was a nightmare.

Half of the equipment in the galley did not work. One air compressor was down. Hot water came in and out, making showers interesting at best. Air conditioning was stuck on a freezing temperature that required bundling up in sweaters and coats no one had brought in the rush to escape Submarine Base Number 1, and watchstanders wrapped themselves in blankets to stay warm and alert. Worst of all, they were down to two meals a day; none of the Chinas wanted *Seven* to come into port for resupply, not when intelligence indicated the ULA rebels had left the East China Sea and were closing in on Red Tiger Station.

Captain Yongzheng, who was normally a calm, competent, and steady presence, grew increasingly quiet and distant, leaving more and more daily tasks to Liao. Normally, Liao would revel in a taste of command, but since he was also holding down the engineer's job—Lieutenant Huang had been ashore with his pregnant wife and didn't make it to the boat on time—the extra duties left him dragging his feet. His eyes were heavy, and he couldn't quite remember the last time he'd gotten good sleep, but that wouldn't matter if they found *Changzheng 14*, would it?

China could not weather one of *her* submarines launching missiles on the world. The three-way civil war had ruined her quite enough. Liao was not a political man. He only cared that his nation came out of these wars with a sense of purpose and self, not whether she was communist or not. He just wanted a chance at a decent life.

Today was not that day, however. Today, sonar had a whiff of *Changzheng 14*, the *Jin*-class ballistic missile submarine.

"You're sure it's *Fourteen*?" he asked their sonar officer. They were lucky that sonar had been in the midst of an all-hands maintenance check when the attack came; otherwise, that department would've been as shorthanded as everyone else. Sonar was the only fully staffed area of *Seven*.

"Yes, sir." The sonar officer's eyes were intent on the display as they both leaned over the operators' shoulders. "The sonar signature matches across the board. There's a small bump of sound on the sixty-five hertz line that makes her unique."

"What about *Eighteen*?" Unless the ULA was stupid, the attack sub would not be far away.

Liao desperately hoped for stupid.

"No sign." The sonar officer winced. "But the port-side array is glitching, and our range is not good in these waters. There's a lot of noise."

"Yes, Red Tiger Station is still busy." Liao rubbed his eyes. "They say it will overtake Armistice Station as the largest underwater station in the world."

The sonar officer snorted. "Only if we stop fighting with ourselves."

"Caution, Rui," Liao said in an undertone. One never knew who was listening, particularly with the Chinese roulette of governments. *Seven* still received orders from two governments, and the Taiwanese were involved now that they were chasing a threat to the entire world.

But it was still the communists one had to worry about most. They might kill someone for expressing insufficiently revolutionary thoughts. The republicans were supposed to be better about that, and the Taiwanese were better, still—they at least had a functional government—but there was still no guarantee which side would win. Caution was the correct watch word.

Rui, a short man with a talent for card tricks, shrugged. "It's a wild world, sir."

"That it is."

"Contact is tracking from left to right," Rui said. "They're not very quiet. Sounds like they have mechanical issues. Something's ticking."

Liao sucked in a deep breath. This was an opportunity. *The* opportunity. If *Seven* could sink the missile submarine, they could take the nuclear threat right out of the ULA's hands. His chest was tight as he wiped sweaty palms against his uniform trousers.

"Are they in range?" he all but whispered.

"Almost. Two more miles. Ten minutes at this speed."

Seven was traveling at a hair above six knots. Did Liao dare speed up? She was an old submarine, with a list of problems and broken equipment longer than his arm. Speed meant noise, as their unfriendly compatriot, *Changzheng 14*, proved. No, they were likely to be heard if they sped up. There had been no time to do a proper self-noise test after *Seven* got underway. Submarine Base Number 1 had the sonar range and the equipment, but no one was manning it after the attack, and *Seven*'s towed sonar array had broken years ago.

Liao had personally put in requisitions for the needed parts with two governments. Neither responded.

"Very well." He frowned at the waterfall display. "Can you fix that glitch?"

"Not without pulling into port." Rui shook his head. "I think a connector or two is loose somewhere. Maybe more. We haven't used these systems in over a year, sir."

"I know." There was nothing to be done about that, so Liao squared his shoulders. "I'll tell the captain."

Now came the creeping feeling of trepidation. Captain Yongzheng was...well, he wasn't himself. Was it the idea of killing their countrymen? *Seven* hadn't fired a shot in the civil wars so far, which meant her crew hadn't, either. Come to think of it, Liao didn't know his captain's politics. Which side did he support? He couldn't possibly sympathize with this "Underwater Liberation Army," could he?

No one knew what they wanted. The ULA announced their capture of three submarines—one of which the Taiwanese immediately sank—two days ago. Now they were silent. Terrorists were supposed to provide lists of demands. That was how the world *worked*. There were rules to this kind of thing. Those who stole critical assets and threatened the world with a nuclear holocaust were responsible for telling said world what they wanted. Liao did not like disorganization or events out of order; chaos was not his friend. And these ULA people promised nothing but.

Those worried thoughts took him straight to the captain's stateroom, where the door was open and Captain Yongzheng sat at his desk, slumped in his chair and staring blankly at a tablet.

"Captain?" Liao asked.

Yongzheng turned slowly. "Liao. Come in." He swallowed. "Close the door."

"What's wrong?" Liao could read that dumbstruck expression, and it promised nothing good.

"The ULA has issued their demands." Yongzheng grimaced as he gestured Liao into a chair, which Liao lowered himself into, feeling like his legs were made of wood.

He licked his suddenly dry lips. "What do they want?"

"They have demanded the surrender of all three Chinese governments. If that does not happen—it is safe to say when—they will fire nuclear missiles at Beijing, Shanghai, and Taipei."

Liao had no words. It was like the air had been sucked out of him, leaving nothing but a husk of skin and bones and blood. He needed far too many seconds to speak, blinking rapidly like it would make the world change. "You think they have the launch codes?" he finally managed to ask.

"Dare we assume they do not?" Yongzheng asked.

"No. Of course not." He swallowed. "We have track on *Changzheng 14*. *Eighteen* is nowhere to be found."

"She'll be here. They won't leave the missile sub unattended."

Liao wasn't sure about that. Did the ULA know anything about submarines? Freedom fighters—or terrorists, depending upon who labeled them—were not necessarily mariners. Had they captured some of the crew? Were some of his comrades operating *Fourteen* and *Eighteen* at gunpoint? Liao shuddered.

What would he do if he found himself in that situation? He liked to think he'd have the fortitude to sabotage the ULA, but the threat of death would frighten anyone. Assuming there were real submariners aboard both submarines was smarter. Yet he wasn't certain the ULA would appreciate good tactics or that his compatriots would share those...unless forced.

Unless some were traitors. Was that how the ULA took the base and the submarines?

A cold chill tore through him, and Liao felt himself sway. The world tilted; his head spun, and his stomach heaved. Just thinking of some of their compatriots betraying China, betraying the *world*, like this made him ill. Even with the civil war, even with the chaos consuming their nation, there was no excuse to ally with terrorists. One had to be an utter fool to think using a nuclear weapon would not alter the fate of the world. The fallout alone would be lethal.

"Are you all right, Liao?" Yongzheng asked after a silence that stretched on far too long.

Was anyone all right?

Liao shook himself. "I must be." He sucked in a shuddering breath. "We have a mission to accomplish."

"We do." Yongzheng stood, and Liao watched his captain, his friend, square his shoulders and face the ugly facts. "Let us go sink one of our nation's most powerful assets."

"Is there not another way?" he whispered, thinking of the Chinese prisoners that *had* to be on board *Fourteen*. And *Eighteen*, too, wherever they were.

"No."

Liao sighed but followed his captain. What else could he do? Nerves danced up and down his spine; *Changzheng 14* was a threat to the world. If those terrorists fired...it did not bear thinking of. He could not afford to feel terror. Not now.

Yet his steps felt heavy. He did not want to sink another Chinese submarine. He did not want to kill his fellows. Neither did anyone on the crew, Liao knew. They all had doubts, doubts that were only eclipsed by their fears. Everyone would do their duty, would hunt *Fourteen* until the end. Was that end today? It seemed so. Liao's stomach lurched as he trudged past an electrical load center that was out of order. Had that load center ever worked? Not in his time aboard *Seven*.

They were halfway to *Seven*'s control room when the unseen mass of *Fourteen*—missed by the sonar team due to a hardware glitch on the ancient port-side array—smashed right into *Seven*'s aging hull.

The other attack submarine was traveling at fifteen knots to *Seven*'s six and hit her port broadside at almost ninety degrees. The impact point was just aft of the sail, and while the crew on board *Eighteen* was too inexperienced to plan the maneuver well, the ULA-captured submarine hit *Seven* with a glancing blow that was hard enough to flip the elderly attack submarine into a hard starboard roll. As *Eighteen* scraped over her, their hulls clanging and grinding against one another through the boat's entire three-hundred-and-fifty-six-foot length, metal screeched, bent, and finally broke. Luckily for the ULA, *Eighteen* had a shrouded propulsor, which kept the screw from taking damage, but her rudder did dig into *Seven*'s hull briefly before the two separated.

Aboard *Seven*, chaos reigned. The roll started with a hard lurch to starboard, with abused metal screeching and unsecured equipment cascading to the lowest point, ripping monitors, tools, pipes, and even compressors out of brackets, off shelves, and clean off the deck. That flying or bouncing danger inevitably found a person to crush, and screams of pain quickly filled *Seven*'s people spaces. Water followed.

The submarine was at battle stations, and her watertight doors were all shut. That saved some lives, but not enough. Once the submarine started to roll, there was little way to stop it. Liao found himself crushed against a bulkhead with his captain next to him, listening helplessly to the cries. Someone, somehow, initiated an emergency blow, but by the time *Seven* rocketed to the surface, righting herself through the force of compressed air, darkness had claimed Liao.

He was not alone.

Chapter 4

The World Turned Upside Down

21 May 2040, Exiting the Strait of Malacca

Bluefish was running shallow, both to check the mail and because the Strait of Malacca, hotly contested waterway though it was, was not the deepest chunk of water on the earth. Plus, in this new and now even weirder world, it paid to remain in contact.

"We still at peace?" Bobby asked as he walked into Alex's stateroom.

Alex glanced up at his new XO. Bobby had officially been in the role for a day less than a month, but he was already a lightyear ahead of his predecessors. He'd handled the battle against Rochambeau well, and now Bobby faced potential nuclear holocaust with his usual aplomb. Not bad.

"If you're asking if the armistice is holding, the answer is yes. For now." Alex sat back in his chair and gestured for Bobby to take a seat.

"Two days strong. Wow." Bobby flopped into the other chair like a dying starfish. "I didn't think it would last more than two hours. You think they'll actually start some peace talks while we're hunting these idiots?"

"From your lips to God's ears." Alex shrugged. "Fuck if I know. It's above my paygrade."

Would the Grand Alliance's leadership reach for peace? Could they? With the gallons of blood spent and the millions of dollars in treasure? The sunk-cost fallacy was certainly a factor in modern warfare; its effects had impacted the war in Afghanistan so powerfully that an entire class at the Naval War College focused on the subject. Alex remembered those lectures very well, but he was hardly in a position to effect change on that level. His job wasn't to decide when to make peace. It was to kill the enemy.

Or, in this case, it was to find a group of suicidal fools who didn't mind if they took the world down with them.

His feelings must've shown in his grimace, because Bobby asked: "Something wrong, Captain?"

"Just thinking about how goddamned stupid you have to be to think tossing a nuclear weapon at a city is a sound idea." Alex shook his head. "Even if no one retaliated—which, by some fucking miracle, might actually happen since the warring powers *all* signed onto this emergency armistice—the fallout would be devastating. Every one of the twelve JL-3s that boat carries has three multiple re-entry vehicles. Every one of *those* has a 150 *kiloton* warhead. That's ten times the power of the bomb that flattened Hiroshima. That's ten times as many people killed *and* ten times as many who will get schwacked by radiation. Ten times as much land will get irradiated. And that's just one of the MRVs. Multiply that times three."

"Thirty times as bad as the worst bomb dropped in history, yeah, pretty picture, loving this." Bobby made a face. "But they can't be that crazy, can they? To actually use a nuke?"

"I hope to hell they aren't, but we've got to treat them like they are."

"They've got to know that China won't surrender," Bobby replied.

Alex snorted. "Which China?"

"Kind of my point. There's three of them, and one of them is diametrically opposed to the others for a list of reasons as long as my arm, but we'll stick with the whole communist thing. There's no way in hell all three Chinese governments will surrender. Not even with Beijing, Shanghai, and Taipei threatened. Tiawan is confident in their ballistic missile defenses, and rightly so. The two Chinas may or may not have assets that can detect and shoot down a missile in time. Either way, none of them are giving in to these demands."

"I wish I could say this isn't our problem, but if someone goes nuclear..." Bobby outlined a mushroom cloud with his hands. "It becomes a game everyone can play."

"And then we're all toast, yeah." Alex's smile was anything but happy; he felt it pulling at the edges of his face like a lead weight. God, he was tired. And this? This was just one more impossible task, one more mission stacked up on top of those he and his crew had already completed, one more time the navy expected him—Alex Coleman, a skinny introvert from Connecticut who didn't know how not to mouth off—to save the day.

Shit. They wanted him to save the goddamned *world* this time.

Alex hadn't signed up for this. He'd just wanted one chance at command of a submarine, one chance to prove he had what it took. After staring the end of his career in the face for far too long—all for doing the right thing and trying to *stop* a war—Alex had never thought he'd see the inside of a sub again. Now, in his second boat, he had somehow become a bona fide hero and the navy's go-to submarine captain.

It was not a comfortable position, but here he was: on a mission to stop terrorists from firing nuclear missiles at three major Chinese cities. How had he of all people ended up here? The last two years had been such a whirlwind that even Alex wasn't always sure.

"Speaking of demands, you see these guys' website?" Bobby pulled up the page on his tablet. "They grew out of the National Socialism Association. They're some whacky splinter group in Taiwan and fascist as all out."

"Really?" Alex felt his eyebrows shoot up. "The name 'Underwater Liberation Army' sounds Marxist."

"Not these boys and girls. They worship Chiang Kai-shek and think a military dictatorship is the only way to reunite China."

"Well, isn't that just ducky." Alex groaned.

"Oh, it gets worse. Check this out. They want to 're-store traditional Chinese values,' criminalize interracial marriage, and they blame democracy for all of Taiwan's problems."

"They sound like real charmers." Alex glanced at the tablet and regretted it; the NSA-ULA website was chock full of propaganda and fascist imagery overlaid on pretty pictures of the ocean.

"Just the kind of people my mom wanted me to bring home for dinner, yeah."

"Just don't invite them on board," Alex said.

"Might be better than where they are," Bobby replied. "We still getting that liaison from one of the democratic Chinas?"

"Yeah, we're due to pick up someone from the Democratic Republic of China off Balabac." Alex glanced at his computer screen to refresh himself on the details. Balabac was the southwestern-most island in the Philippines, a longtime American ally and junior member of the Grand Alliance. "They opened relations with the mainland DROC months ago, apparently."

"Glad to know someone isn't too busy shooting. When do we pick him or her up?"

"He'll be there tomorrow. We're about a thousand nautical miles out, so you tell me the nav plan, mister not-so-navigator."

Bobby slumped in his chair. "Somehow, it always comes back to that job. It's like an ex-girlfriend who just won't leave." He sighed. "I'll get Rene to work up the plan. Looking at the time-distance, we should need a day and a half or so? I don't think we want to sprint around in waters this busy if we can avoid it."

"No, thanks. I'd rather hear it coming if we're going to drive up under the belly of some merchant and involuntarily mate with them."

Bobby snickered, but even a joke didn't lessen the feeling of leaden pressure between Alex's shoulder blades. Yes, he had a Chinese liaison on the way—however much good that would do. Yes, he had a good boat and the best crew in the world. But so had Jules Rochambeau. One look at the statistics told Alex he was living on borrowed time. One day, perhaps soon, he'd screw up.

And one mistake would be all it took to send *Bluefish* to the bottom.

Four days of sprinting and drifting brought *Andromeda* three quarters of the way to her destination and left Captain Revnik significantly happier than she was upon leaving the Seychelles. She was particularly relieved that there was no Camille Dubois here to grumble non-stop about Rochambeau's capture, which, *yes*, Katerina agreed was a blow to the ULP, yet one would think Dubois was in love with the man from the way she nattered on. Katerina had met the man, however. *No thank you* had been her repeated refrain until she'd threatened to break his too-perfect nose. Was Rochambeau the best of the best? Probably.

Maybe. Katerina aimed to be better now that she had a submarine that could take the war to the enemy in ways that her first boat could not. She was past feeling shame for *Kazan's* sinking. First, because Rochambeau *also* going down to Coleman left her in good company. Second, she had executed a good trap and captured an enemy submarine. Who else could claim that laurel? To her knowledge, the Grand Alliance *still* didn't know that particular Australian diesel submarine wasn't on the bottom, and Katerina Revnik would not be the one to tell them.

Now they were at peace. She wasn't sure what to make of that. Katerina was made for war, and while she knew she could excel during peacetime...what was she supposed to do with this marvelous submarine if the shooting stopped? Play war games and show the flag in foreign ports while Russia scrambled for diplomatic purchase? Her nation deserved to be a world power again, not to be the comical bad guy who civilized nations looked down upon.

The thought must've made her hiss aloud, because her second-in-command turned to face her. "Captain? Is everything all right?"

Captain Third Rank Daniil Zhukov was Katerina's opposite in every way save those that mattered. He was tall, built like a solid tree, while her slender figure betrayed her as the former figure skater she'd been. Katerina had beautiful and angular features, contrasting with Zhukov's face, which looked like it had been run over by a truck that came back for seconds. He was quiet where she was outgoing, too, but they were both professionals with sound tactical minds. More importantly, the months working up *Andromeda* told Katerina they made a good team.

"I do not trust this peace," she said after a long moment. "This Grand Alliance might come to some agreement with France, but they will do everything they can to ruin Russia's chances of rising again."

"*Da.* There is no chance they give us favorable terms." Zhukov grimaced. "Do you think our leadership agrees?"

"No doubt." She sat back in her chair, her gaze sweeping over *Andromeda's* empty wardroom. As the third ship in a new class, as well as the first submarine with her name, there were few hand-me-down decorations on the walls. But she treasured the beautiful painting of *Andromeda* by an up-and-coming Russian artist...as well as the signed and framed comic book cover for the first issue of *Here We Stand.*

Here We Stand was a new comic book, centered on Russian submariners fighting against the Grand Alliance. Would that vanish in the deadly maw of peace, too? Katerina hoped not, although she admitted to herself that it was for selfish reasons.

She was one of the three submarine captains chosen to be models for the comics...and of the other two, only Dimitry Kovalev remained alive.

Dimitry Kovalev was an annoyance. She could admit that in the privacy of her own mind, too. His sudden success should not be a threat, but Katerina still wished he were a bit less flamboyant about it. The comic book had already created an arc based on his actions off of Alaska, and the Russian public loved it. They had been too long without wholesome heroes.

The next arc would belong to her. She would make sure of that.

"Do you think we will continue the war if peace holds?" Zhukov asked.

Katerina licked her lips. "I suspect as much, but I am not certain. I am not sure America will let go, either. Their international standing has been severely damaged. They need a major victory or the United States will no longer be a superpower."

"Can we hope for that much?" Zhukov smiled. "A multi-power world is more stable. Every strategist knows that."

She laughed. "Except the American ones, apparently."

"Would finding this stolen missile submarine be the victory they need?" Zhukov stroked his chin. "I assume they've sent Coleman after it."

"They'd be fools not to." Katerina did not voice her desire to meet the man. That would not be patriotic, even if it was merely for professional reasons. She sighed. "He is a canny enemy. I should know."

Zhukov was not crass enough to mention *Kazan's* sinking. "I have read the reports on him. He seems smart."

"We will have to be on our toes to beat him," Katerina replied. "But it is what Russia needs. You are right; we must deny them this victory, or else the peace may last and America may rise from the ashes of their stupidity."

"Then we will find the Chinese rebels first and sink them."

Katerina hoped it would be that simple.

Chapter 5

The Calm

23 May 2040, Red Tiger Station

"Color me delighted about being back here," Alex muttered as *Bluefish's* sailors received lines from the TRANSPLAT number three on the world's second largest underwater station.

On the surface, everything looked peaceful. Almost like the world really wasn't pretending the armistice would hold and delay the war; people moved around without weapons in hand, laughing and joking, and station security had decreased significantly since Alex's last visit. Was that smart? He had no idea. The last time he'd been to Red Tiger Station, the surrounding waters had been a pirate's paradise, with easy access to expensive ships and even more expensive cargo. Even Alex's first submarine, the aging *Jimmy Carter*, had been interesting enough to target.

Yeah, he had a great big love for this place. Coming back was fantastic. Particularly when they weren't even *supposed* to be here. Their liaison was supposed to meet them in the Philippines, but last-minute changes brought everyone back to Alex's second-favorite underwater station.

"I don't know, I hear that Red Tiger Station put in a glass-bottomed swimming pool where you can see the ocean and feel like you're swimming with sea creatures," Bobby replied around the lollipop in his mouth.

Alex snorted. "You understand that's what SCUBA diving is for. Then you *can* swim with sea creatures. For real." He missed diving. The last time Alex got any quality time with fins and a tank was before the war started.

"What about the aquatic light show? I hear they're calling it the tenth wonder of the world."

"Sure, maybe that'll make a better memory than the riots I dealt with when *Jimmy Carter* was here," Alex replied.

"Gee, Captain, it sure seems like you're holding Ursula North levels of grudge here."

Alex mock glared at his XO. "I could only *aspire* to her level of fury and damnation. She holds grudges like it's an art form."

Bobby snickered. "Sounds like you need to get cracking, sir. You've got a lot of catching up to do."

Alex rolled his eyes. "Sounds like you need to get on the horn and find out where our liaison is. I have no intention of staying in this place any longer than necessary."

"You want to put down liberty call in the meantime? It's peace and all."

Frowning, Alex scanned the workers milling about on the piers sticking out of the TRANSPLAT like long spindles. Even upon second glance, none seemed armed, which really wasn't that different now that he thought about it; last time Alex was here, Red Tiger Station was barely able to defend itself. The pirates had ruled and the residents and personnel of the station were left stranded. Now, however, most of the workers seemed engaged in maintenance or servicing ships alongside the piers. Basically, they were doing their jobs. Still, Alex watched them for too long, waiting for something to go wrong or for shooting to start.

Maybe he was paranoid. Maybe he'd been at war too long.

"Yeah." Alex tried not to chew his lower lip and failed. "Let's do it. We're scheduled to be here for two days, so let 'em have some fun. Normal rules apply. There's no guarantee anything's safe around here."

"You got it, sir."

Bobby vanished down the ladder, leaving Alex to stare at the pier alone. Worry prickled up his spine like an invisible insect crawling upward inch by inch, but he pushed it away. The armistice was holding. The world was at peace, however tenuous.

Peace was lovely, presuming one could ignore the looming approach of doomsday. He drummed his fingers against the warming metal of *Bluefish's* sail's edge, watching a Chinese destroyer approach the next pier to the right. Was their liaison on board? Alex pushed aside the need to fidget. His earliest years in the navy had been consumed by the expectation of war with China. War against other powers had been unexpected, as had China's internal implosions. Did a closeup view of a Chinese warship encourage those old animosities to bubble up? Perhaps.

Perhaps Alex was just annoyed that he didn't know which of the three Chinas that ship belonged to. Or if this Undersea Liberation Army had bagged themselves a destroyer, too. He wasn't sure which class that puppy was, but that ship sure looked like a late model *Arleigh Burke*-class. Good on China for stealing American technology, he supposed. Now that was likely in terrorist hands, too.

His phone rang, making Alex jump. He'd forgotten there was service here. A quick check told him that it was his least favorite person calling—or maybe his second least favorite, right after Admiral Hamilton. Alex grimaced and decided he couldn't get away with pretending he'd left his phone below.

"Captain Coleman speaking, how may I help you, sir?"

"This is Commodore Banks," his boss said. The edge in Banks's voice was clear enough to jerk Alex up short; just because he and Banks didn't like each other didn't mean he expected his superior to be confrontational from moment one.

"What can I do for you today, sir?" Alex asked, forcing his voice to remain even.

How quickly could he get off this call if he agreed with everything Banks said? He knew Banks didn't like his tactics, his leadership style, and quite possibly his wife, too. Nancy was better at playing nice with senior officers possessing a terminal case of stupidity, but even she was sick of this officious dickweed.

Fuck, he shouldn't label Banks like that, even in the privacy of his own mind. Sooner or later, his mouth would run away with that idea and spit something out to Banks's face.

"This is Commodore Banks. I'd like you to report your status immediately."

"As reported via message, we arrived pierside at Red Tiger Station about an hour ago." That was the closest Alex could get to telling his boss to *read the official message traffic captains were required to send* without calling him an idiot out loud.

Banks, of course, ignored him. "Good. Moving on, I'd like to remind you that we are now at *peace* and shooting any anyone other than your assigned targets would be a gross violation of naval regulations *and* international law."

"I am aware of that, thank you, sir." Keeping his tone polite was a challenge.

"It would *also* be considered an act of war by our former enemies. I am certain you have no interest in re-sparking a globe-spanning war, particularly after your previous experiences."

Not throwing the phone into the water was hard. The navy paid for the damn thing; surely Alex could claim it was an accident. And losing a cell phone would be better for his career than telling Banks what he thought of his goddamned insinuations.

Banks didn't like him, fine. He didn't approve of Alex's so-called "cowboy" tactics—which were not born of a desire for fame so much as a pressing need to keep fucking living and maybe even kill the enemy *like his job required*. What the hell had caused this?

"My *previous experiences*, as you call them, were wrapped around trying to *stop* World War III, not start it," Alex replied, his voice tight. "I understand the potentially catastrophic repercussions of shooting at any submarine other than my targets during the armistice." He paused to bit back the colorful litany of swear words that came to mind.

"That's good to hear, Captain. I trust you'll keep it in mind moving forward. The world is counting on you." Banks's sneer was damn near audible. "As Admiral Rodriquez was quick to remind me this morning."

Ah. He was stuck in the middle of a pissing contest again, wasn't he? Banks hated *his* boss even more than he hated Alex, which was worth something, Alex supposed. At least he had Rodriquez's confidence?

"We're all aware of the pressure, sir." Alex was glad Banks couldn't see his face; he was no smooth political operator, and he was constitutionally incapable of hiding his feelings. "We're still on track and are awaiting our Chinese liaison. I expect to get underway tomorrow evening."

"And have you received said liaison yet?" There Banks went, showing off his lack of reading comprehension yet again.

Had Alex included this information in the message sent just forty-four minutes ago? Of course he had.

"Negative." Alex hated repeating himself when the idiot on the other end couldn't be bothered to listen. "Our local contact says he should arrive by close of business."

"Then why are you remaining at the station longer than that? Surely you understand the need for haste in a situation such as this."

"My stores onload could not be scheduled earlier than zero eight hundred." Fucking A, could this man not be bothered to read *anything*? Alex reconsidered yeeting the phone into the South China Sea. He did not mention that he planned to allow a third of the crew—today's duty section, which would not get liberty due to the requirement to remain on the boat—to skip helping with the stores onload so they could enjoy the station a little. He was sure Banks would not approve. The commodore had never demonstrated that he gave rat's ass about crew morale. Instead, Alex took a deep breath. Raging at his squadron commander would only put him on a course toward the shoals. "Assuming it arrives on time, I will be underway on schedule."

"I dislike prevarication, Captain," Banks replied. "Your mission is of the *utmost importance*. The world is at stake. If the

United States does not destroy that rogue missile submarine, the world might tumble back into war."

"Sir, I dislike the implication that you believe I will do one iota less than my duty." Not swearing at the asshole was almost impossible.

"Your opinion is noted."

As is your lack of tactical aptitude, Alex didn't say. Had he ever gotten good advice or decent orders from this man? Instead of contemplating that answer, he imagined Banks trying to complete this mission with whatever submarine he'd commanded a dog's age ago. Ineptitude all around! He growled out a sigh.

"Is there anything else I can do for you, Commodore?" he asked.

"Not at this time. The squadron will check in with you again tomorrow afternoon. I expect you to be underway by then."

"If it's not tomorrow afternoon Zulu, I recommend you be prepared for disappointment," Alex replied before he could stop himself.

Yeah, there his mouth went again. Fuck.

"I'll make note of that, *Captain*," Banks snapped.

Sure, make note of that, Alex didn't say. Nothing short of setting off his *own* nuclear weapon would damage his career. He was a goddamned Medal of Honor winner. Alex Coleman might as well be ten feet tall and bullet proof for all the damage Banks could do to his fitness report.

"Is there anything else?" Alex asked without an ounce of the regret he should be feeling. "If not, I have a submarine to replenish and a liaison to meet."

"No, that is all. I can see you have nothing else to communicate. Good day, Captain."

"Good day."

Alex hung up before Banks could say more. The headache pounding behind his eyes made him want to scream, but he just gritted his teeth, returned his phone to his pocket, and headed below. He had a goddamned submarine to run and war to prevent.

Why the fuck did people like Banks make it so *hard*?

24 May 2040, the South China Sea

Thirty hours after Alex's acrimonious phone call with the SUBRON, *Bluefish* got underway from Red Tiger Station with a Chinese liaison on board. Alex wasn't entirely clear on *which* Chinese navy Commander Liao Fan was from, but he understood that Fan came from the pro-democracy side. That was something.

Commander Fan spoke good English, too, which was why he said he'd been chosen.

"Captain Yongzheng would be here, but you would probably not understand him," Liao said over dinner after *Bluefish* reached the open waters beyond Red Tiger Station. "I understand that our communist counterparts sent someone to work with the Russians as well. Captain Yongzheng offered to sail aboard *Andromeda*, but he does not speak Russian, either. Only Japanese, and they did not send anyone."

"They don't have a lot of boats left to send," Rose replied with her customary bluntness. The Japanese Naval Self-Defense Force had been decimated by Russia in the early days of the war, and so far, rebuilding had proven a challenge. Two years after the worst of it, Japan owned a handful of German export U-Boats. They were older models, despite having AIP technology, and no one expected the Japanese to throw them into the line of fire.

Liao flushed. "We don't get a that much news in Jianggezhuang."

"Small wonder why," Rose said around a mouth full of french fries. "You've been a little busy with your own war. Wars?"

"It feels like several." Liao frowned. "But please understand that these terrorists—this Undersea Liberation Army—does not represent China. Not our navy and not our people."

Even Rose wasn't impolite enough to mention there were several Chinas going on at the moment. No one in the wardroom thought *any* of the Chinas wanted to set off a nuclear weapon. They weren't suicidal. Terrorists and rebels, on the other hand...

Yeah. Alex didn't *like* thinking about what could happen if those idiots launched even one nuclear missile. Sure, the fallout would be less than most science fiction writers speculated—even though the *Jin* carried MRVs, or multiple reentry vehicles, which meant each individual missile could hit multiple targets—but it would still be horrible. If they did hit multiple cities in China, most of Asia would feel either the physical or economic fallout. The rest of the world would only get the latter.

But that wasn't the worst of it. If someone started lobbing nuclear missiles around, where would it stop? The cultural horror from bombing Nagasaki and Hiroshima still lingered in most of humanity, but once one power crossed the threshold, everyone knew the carnage would only grow from there. Russia had held back so far. China showed restraint even in the face of a three-way civil war. The United States had no appetite for nuking *another* country, nor did the rest of her allies in the Grand Alliance. France was supposedly civilized. India was more of a wildcard, having never fought in a knock-down, drag-out world war before, but no one actually thought they'd be stupid enough to shoot. Every world leader feared the consequences of pulling that particular trigger.

The first to fire a nuke would lose. Everyone knew that. The rest of the world would turn on that nation, war or no war.

But what if someone else launched a nuke? What then? Who would follow?

"No one thinks that, promise," Bobby replied to Liao and broke into Alex's thoughts. "We all know we've got to catch a couple of crazies. This isn't *The Hunt for Red October*."

Liao's smile was small. "I've read that book."

"I think it's required reading for submariners. Even if it's old, it's good." Bobby grinned. "Even Rosie here doesn't hate it, and she hates most submarine books on principle."

"Most *navy* books suck donkey balls," Rose replied. "They never—"

"You had to get her started, didn't you, Bobby?" Lou cut in. "We know, we know. Navy books and movies always portray sailors and officers wrong. Everyone's popping to attention and saluting for no reason, not to mention officers yelling at everyone."

Rose rolled her eyes. "Thanks for stealing my thunder."

"As the only person at this table who was ever a drill instructor, I maintain that my right to complain is greater than yours." Lou sat back, his expression serene. "I concur. The genre caters to armchair experts, not the actual military. Clancy aside."

"If I may turn the topic back to our targets," Alex said, raising his voice to talk over Bobby's snickering and Rose's muttering, "I'd like to hear what happened to your submarine."

Liao paled. "*Changzheng-7* was rammed. *Changzheng-18*—one of what you would call a *Shang*-class—escaped detection. I am not sure how. Maybe our sonar systems were not operating at full capacity. *Seven* was commissioned in 2006."

Several people whistled; that made *Seven* thirty-four years old, older than every submarine in the U.S. Navy except *Virginia*. Sure, they'd recommissioned some of the *Los Angeles*-class boats, but those had spent years in mothballs and were thoroughly upgraded. From the sounds of things, *Seven* hadn't had those advantages.

Alex caught Bobby's eyes on him and smiled wryly. *Seven* had been about *Jimmy Carter's* age, but it sounded like his first boat made a better accounting for herself at the end. At least she'd lived to bring his crew home, even if she'd been cut up into thousands of very expensive razor blades last year.

"Did the other boat survive?" Alex asked.

"She did not surface. I do not think she rolled over like we did, either." Liao grimaced. "So, yes, I think she must have.

Although I cannot imagine she is very quiet now. I think her rudder caught our hull."

"That should screw with her maneuverability." Bobby scratched his chin.

"It won't help us much if she's on course for ramming," Alex replied. "The HY-80 steel on this baby won't stand up to that. She'll crack right open."

"Gee, that's a happy thought, Captain. Thank you for that," Bobby said.

Alex grinned. "At your service." Then he sobered. "All right, so we need to keep an eye out for aging and loud *Shangs* while we're looking for the *Jin*. At least Taiwan took out the other one for us."

"I think *Eighteen* must be damaged," Liao said. "What you call *Shangs* are not sturdy enough to withstand that without consequences."

"That's good to know," Rose said. "Maybe we'll need fewer torpedoes, as it seems like our squadron doesn't give a fuck if we get enough."

"Easy there, Rose," Lou said in an undertone before Bobby or Alex had to speak up.

She glared but subsided. "My point still stands. Maybe one fish will do her in when we find her."

"You are so confident you will do so?" Liao asked.

Rose shrugged. "Our luck says we'll find them both right in the thick of everything dangerous. Welcome to *Bluefish*."

"Hey, at least our luck no longer says we'll claim to be broken and stay pierside," Lou said. When Liao threw him a questioning look, Lou added: "Our last captain wasn't fond of action."

"How can you not be in war?" Liao cocked his head.

"Great question. I wish we'd figured it out," Bobby replied. Alex almost thanked him out loud but thought better of it. No one needed to hear Rose call the commodore's best friend a coward, even if it was true.

"I see." Liao frowned. "I do not think that is a problem with *Eighteen*. They hit us at speed. As for *Fourteen*, the, how do you call it, 'boomer?' She did not take action. Perhaps that crew is less aggressive."

"One can only hope," Alex said.

"Their threats certainly aren't," Rose put in.

"No," Liao replied. "That is why we were sent to kill them." He gestured vaguely at *Bluefish* with one hand. "And why it is your turn now, I suppose."

"Your unfortunate experience tells us what to look out for." Alex leaned back and steepled his fingers. "Now we have to figure out where to find them, lest we end up bumbling around the South China like a blindfolded fool."

"Ah, I always wanted to be Odysseus, Captain." Bobby's eyes sparkled.

"Speak for yourself," Lou replied. "I prefer Patroclus myself."

"Ugh, did you people actually read that?" Rose scowled. "I read the *For Dummies* version in high school. I was too busy playing volleyball."

Her comment kicked off a debate over the literary merits of epic poetry, but Alex barely listened. His mind was full of ideas concerning how to avoid being rammed by one submarine while sneaking up on another. Enemies who wanted to sink him were easier. These ULA fellows were something else.

But failure was not an option, was it?

Chapter 6

Unlikely Friends

THE WORLD HOLDS ITS BREATH

Mark Easley, Washington Post

MAY 24TH—Are we awaiting Armageddon? With a ballistic missile submarine and its twenty-plus nuclear missiles under the control of terrorists or freedom fighters, it seems like no one knows. An armistice was declared, but beyond that, what are world governments doing?

No one knows.

When asked what actions the U.S. Navy is taking to combat this threat, Commander Seth Kobialka, spokesman for Commander, Submarine Forces Pacific, replied that "current submarine operations remain classified and cannot be briefed to the press." When asked if the U.S. Navy has even deployed anyone to face this threat, he simply gave a "no comment" that tells the world absolutely nothing. Only Russia seems eager to share their participation; state-owned television stations are reporting that Russia's premier submarine, *Andromeda*, is on the case.

This seems like an odd time to depend upon Russia to save us. Less than a week ago, Russians were shooting at—and killing—Americans. While everyone should value and pursue this chance at peace, trusting former enemies will take time. Is there any coordination between Russian and American forces? What about the Chinese, who lost this submarine (and others)? No one seems to know.

Tension on the home front is high. There have been protests in multiple large cities by people who fear the Undersea Liberation Army will strike American cities. Multiple action groups have demanded answers from the government, but none have been forthcoming.

Will the ULA fire those missiles? Will they be stopped by Russia or one of the many Chinese forces? The world is still holding its breath.

Scowling, Alex put his tablet down on the wardroom table. Its plain metal case contrasted sharply with the blue vinyl table cover; the tablet was a hallmark of the navy finally embracing twenty-first century technology, whereas that same blue vinyl had been used in the *last* world war. Some things didn't change, did they? He felt his scowl deepen. Mark Easley was definitely one of those things. His *Post* article hadn't said anything groundbreaking, they weren't *wrong*...yet the article still rankled.

"You read the Easley article?" Bobby asked between bites of pancake coated in enough syrup to make a teenager pause. "I see that look on your face."

"Am I that obvious?"

"Like a snowman in the desert."

He snorted. "I'm not so fond of this Easley dude. I remember his hit piece after the *Kansas* Incident. Living through that was a fucking joy."

"Sounds like. We were well clear of that clusterfuck, of course. Can't have *Bluefish* where the fire is hottest, even before the war," Bobby replied.

"Jesus, Bobby." Shaking his head, Alex sat back in his chair. One could always trust his XO to blurt out inconvenient truths, such as the fact that Alex's predecessor had avoided action like the proverbial plague.

Alex didn't understand that mindset. He'd spent the first year of the war *praying* for just one chance to prove he and his crew had what it took to take the fight to the enemy. Of course, getting that chance almost proved fatal, when the Indians attacked the lightly defended Convoy 57, sank almost all of the escorts, and left *Jimmy Carter* alone to face overwhelming odds. They'd somehow survived chasing the enemy off, but it had been a near thing.

Yet here he was, still dancing the dance and doing his best to serve his country. Thinking about Peterson's reasoning just did not compute. Why put the uniform on only to shy away from doing their duty? Now Peterson was doing whatever he was doing, and *Bluefish* was out to save the world.

Just thinking of what one nuclear missile could do to that world left wild butterflies screaming about in Alex's stomach.

"I'm here to serve, Captain." Bobby grinned.

"I bet you are."

"You know, there are times—" Alex cut off as the phone to his right rang. On *Cero*-class submarines, there was a phone installed right next to the captain's right thigh, and damn was that convenient in moments like this. He snatched it. "Captain."

"Good morning, sir, it's Weps," Lieutenant Rose Lange said. "I have the deck and we have a contact bearing two-five-fiver, range ten thousand yards. Sonar says tonals match a *Pictor*-class submarine."

Alex sat up straight. "Well, that sounds like an interesting peacetime wrinkle. What's their course and speed?"

"They're on a roughly parallel heading, speed twenty-nine knots."

"Someone isn't worried about being heard." He chewed his lip. The range was closer than he liked...but the world was at peace. "I'll be right there."

"You want to go to battle stations?" Rose asked.

"Nah. It's peace, remember?"

"You say so, sir. We'll continue to monitor."

"Very well." Alex hung up and looked at his XO. "Want to join the fun? Looks like we've got a *Pictor* rolling into the game."

Bobby whistled. "Those *Pictors* are supposed to be hot shit. Maybe we can at least grab some good intel? Even peacetime navies like intel, right?" He cocked his head. "We've been at war so long that I'm forgetting what that's like."

Alex chuckled as he rose. "It's amazing how war can make two years feel like an eternity, yeah."

Would this be it? Would World War III top out at two years, or would the disparate enemies find ways to keep fighting? Alex was no historian, but he still enjoyed reading military history, and the Naval War College had taught him to look at the root causes for conflicts.

Unfortunately, doing that left a queasy feeling in the pit of his stomach that didn't vanish on the short walk to control. Dozens of competing claims to territory on the ocean floor hadn't been resolved. Territory taken by both sides hadn't been given back, and some of that territory included islands whose natives didn't want to become part of another nation. Underwater stations were easier; most of their owners and residents would accept a payment—or bribe—to leave and never come back if they didn't like the new management. But nations did not appreciate conquest.

There'd been a time when people believed that the United Nations could stop another world war. That *talking* to one another would resolve problems and the UN would be able to mediate anything reasonable nations could not work out. Conquest was a thing of the past, as was colonialization; both were considered dead, right alongside the end of the British Empire. But when Russia's invasions of Ukraine in the early twenty-first century were largely left unanswered...thinking started to shift.

Now here they were, clinging to a flimsy armistice that made no attempt to address why France and India had claimed so much territory, why Russia was doing the same to Japanese islands and stations, or why tensions were so high that an American admiral flat out shot the wrong submarine on day one of the war. Alex was glad for the armistice, he was, but that agreement wrapped around the nuclear threat.

What would happen when that threat was vanquished?

Alex entered control with Bobby on his heels, his gaze flicking around the space through force of habit. Fire control and weapons were to the left, ship control—or helm and ballast control, in the old parlance that won out again in the *Cero*-class—were up forward, and navigation plus the electronics technicians were to the right. Radio and sonar both had their own spaces attached to control; in the case of radio, it was a tiny closet. Sonar was a bit bigger. Unlike wartime, the curtains to both spaces were open.

Lieutenant Rose Lange held the watch as officer of the deck, and she stood next to the navigation/tactical table in the center, where the input from all of *Bluefish's* sensors was synergized into one display. The originals of that ilk on *Virginia* and her sisters had been touchscreens, but sailors could break anything, so they'd installed a trackball and replaced the sensitive-but-breakable screen. As always, Rose was zeroed into her target with the merciless precision of a smart torpedo; now, she glared at Chief Andreas, whose presence outside the sonar room stirred up an uneasy feeling in Alex's gut.

"How're we looking?" He stuffed his hands in his pockets.

"That *Pictor* is closer than I like." Rose made a face. "I know we say we're at peace, Captain, but five nautical miles and closing is a bit personal for people who were shooting at us last week."

"Closing? I thought they were on a parallel course?"

"They turned." Rose's scowl deepened.

"They had to be moving slow before, Captain, or we'd have heard them," Andreas said. "The tail's out and we're only at ten knots. No way could they storm up on us at that speed."

"You think they know something we don't know?" Bobby asked from behind Alex's left shoulder. "Did the shooting start again?"

"At ten thousand yards, they'd have shot already," Alex replied. "The Russians sure as hell aren't in the business of giving their newest and shiniest boats to morons."

Bobby snickered. "That's a pity."

"Yeah, well, now this guy's acting like they want to make friends. *Good* friends, if you know what I mean," Rose replied. "They're CBDR."

Constant Bearing, Decreasing Range, or CBDR, was a shiphandler's way of saying that a collision was unavoidable if neither vessel changed course or speed. Underwater collisions had happened over the years, including a famous one between a British and a French submarine before the war. The U.S. Navy didn't admit to most of their near misses, particularly those during the Cold War, but everyone in uniform knew they'd happened.

Adding himself and his boat to that undistinguished list was not an accomplishment Alex wanted to add to his resume.

Nor was getting hit by one of those legendary three-hundred-knot torpedoes. Long held to be just a thing of rumor, more and more reports of ultra-high speed Russian torpedoes destroying Alliance submarines had surfaced, leaving even skeptics like Alex convinced of their existence. But the rules of engagement were different during an armistice. This was peace...right?

Two weeks ago, Alex would've had two torpedoes in the water already. Today, he stepped on the instinct to shoot and forced himself to wait.

The international rules of the road said that the *Pictor* was the stand-on vessel, though Alex couldn't think of *any* time when those rules had been followed underwater. Plus, the rules of the road specifically applied to vessels *in sight of one another*, which they definitely weren't. Life wasn't some sci-fi movie where submarines had windows and could see into the abyss.

"Come left fifteen degrees," Alex ordered. He didn't want to lose their forward momentum, but a slight turn would open the range and keep *Bluefish* on track. "Let's try some manners on for size."

Bobby snickered. "Do the Russians know what those are?"

"Doubtful," Rose said, relaying the orders to the helm.

Alex shrugged. "We don't have time to educate them. The mission is to find that Chinese boomer, not fuck about with the Russians."

"Ah, Captain, that's not far. That's what we do best." Bobby grinned as *Bluefish* shifted course.

"I'd say we're better at making the French miserable, but that doesn't mean we shouldn't branch out," Rose said.

The crew in control laughed, Alex included. It was true that *Bluefish* had probably done more damage to French submarines and French morale, but there was still time. Assuming the war continued.

Alex cocked his head at the plot. Yeah, the Russians were probably here for the same purpose as *Bluefish*. There'd been no update from the squadron confirming if any other nation intended to send subs after the rogue missile sub, but given

Commodore Banks's gracious call a few days ago, Alex wasn't surprised by the dearth of information on that front. Not after that charming interaction.

"Conn, Sonar, we have an incoming Gertrude call." Chief Andreas's voice made Alex twist to stare at the internal intercom that sailors from the beginning of time had nicknamed the bitch box.

Blinking, he keyed the microphone to ask: "Sonar, Captain, say again?"

The Gertrude was a submarine's underwater telephone. Although numerous technological updates now allowed submarines to talk to surface ships and aircraft from underwater, the classic Gertrude was at least as old as the last world war. Every submarine still monitored those frequencies, even if they almost never used them. That was probably why Chief Andreas sounded as mystified as Alex felt.

"Incoming Gertrude call, sir. Sounds Russian. Net five."

"What the fuck?" Alex twisted to turn a nearby speaker and associated handset to the specified voice net. Sure enough, he caught the transmission mid-sentence.

"—submarine, presumably *Bluefish*, this is the Russian attack submarine *Andromeda* calling you on underwater telephone, over."

The message repeated while Alex tamed his eyebrows; they wanted to do a jig, and that wasn't professional. Then he grabbed the handset, pushing aside the echo of his old hatred of public speaking.

"This is *Bluefish*, roger, over," he said. Procedure said that the names of operational submarines were classified, but *Andromeda* had already spoiled the surprise for anyone within Gertrude range.

Thankfully, they had no sonar contacts that close, except for this mysterious Russian. Not letting his heart beat out of his chest was so damned hard, and no one was even shooting.

"This is *Andromeda* Actual," an accented female voice said, speaking very good English. "May I speak to Captain Coleman, please?"

"You know you've made it when even the bad guys call you by name, Captain," Bobby said as Alex stared at the Gertrude handset for a long moment.

Goddamn it all; Bobby was right. Alex still wasn't sure how he felt about being the Alliance's go-to submarine captain...but here he was. They'd been sent after Rochambeau. Now they were on the hunt for this stolen missile boat. A shuddering chill ran down his spine. Alex wasn't always sure how he'd gotten here, even if he could look back on his recent career and explain every moment. No one wanted him to become a rock star. Navy leaders didn't like brash submarine commanders who couldn't control their big honking mouths...yet here he was, about to talk to a Russian submarine captain like it was just every other Tuesday.

Alex took a deep breath before keying the mic. "This *Bluefish* Actual, roger, over."

"*Bluefish* this is *Andromeda*. It is nice to finally speak to you," the other voice replied. "We met before when I commanded *Kazan*, and I must compliment you on not falling for my trap."

"Oh, *fuck*," Alex whispered. This was Katerina Revnik. Before *Bluefish* sent *Kazan* to the bottom, that sub—and Revnik—had laid mines and lured another boat into a trap, allowing Russia to take an Australian diesel boat *and* her crew intact. Good luck would've taken Revnik to the bottom with *Kazan*, but he wasn't supposed to think that way when there wasn't a war on.

"We sank her, didn't we?" Bobby asked.

"Yep." Shaking his head at the absurdity of the universe, Alex lifted the handset again. "I'll take that compliment in the spirit it was intended, *Andromeda*," he said. "Am I correct in guessing that we are allies while searching for this rogue boomer, over?"

"*Da*. It seems fate has a sense of humor," Revnik replied. "I have a proposition. If you line up a better shot on the missile submarine, we will sink the attack boat...and vice versa? Do you concur, over?"

"I'll be damned." Alex muttered the words without keying the microphone. But only needed a split second to make this decision. "*Bluefish* concurs, over."

"We're working with the *Russians?*" Rose clearly couldn't stop her eyes from going wide, and Alex didn't think she'd tried.

"Yep. This isn't a time for national pride or ambition. If ULP fires those missiles, we all lose."

Rose swallowed. "We'll follow your lead, sir."

Alex flashed her a smile of thanks, but he didn't have time to say more before Revnik continued:

"Splendid. This may be the only time we wish you good hunting, *Bluefish*, but we seem as if we are the only ones able to stop this insanity, over."

You're telling me, Alex didn't say. Instead, a snicker bubbled up. "It's a pity we can't come up in Link with you, but I think both our nations would prohibit such sharing," he said into the Gertrude mic.

"Pity indeed." He could hear Revnik's laughter through the scratchy connection. "Perhaps someday."

"Someday. Yeah." Alex grimaced, wondering if the war *would* end here…or if he should just share that track data, anyway. Could he? Two submarines fumbling about in the dark without a good track on one another could just as easily sink a quasi-friend as they could the enemy they hunted for. Shit. Commodore Banks would probably filet him—and his crew—if he did that. Their systems probably weren't compatible, anyway, unless the Russians had stolen more NATO technology than he thought. "Thank you for the call, *Andromeda*. We'll see you around. This is *Bluefish* Actual, out."

"*Andromeda* Actual, roger, out."

Alex stared blankly at the plot as he hung up the handset, his mind whirling. Was this the beginning of peace? Instinct wanted to *like* the person on the other end of that call, but two years of war told him she was the enemy. A professional, smart, and *capable* enemy…who might've been a colleague if the world turned out slightly different. Or might someday be. The Russian navy had come a long way from the wreck they'd been in the post–Cold War world. Usually, he lamented that fact.

Today, it might help save the world.

Chapter 7

Operational Security

26 May 2040, the South China Sea

A day and a half of fruitless searching later—with *Andromeda* never too far away—left *Bluefish's* crew frustrated and on edge. The Russians never again came within a range Alex would've considered rude during peacetime, but they all knew they remained within one another's maximum effective range. Seeing one of Russia's newest and shiniest attack submarines lurking on the edge of their search area left Alex both weirdly comforted and a touch twitchy. However, the fact that they were deep in old-school submarine warfare was far more exhausting.

How had he thought this was *fun* when he was younger? Junior officer Alex Coleman was a fucking idiot. Sure, there was a great challenge in finding a sonar contact that didn't want to be found, but he preferred shooting enemies and getting it the hell over with. It was more efficient, and if he was ashamed to say it was fun, well, maybe the universe shouldn't have made him good at his job.

"You know, Captain, I'm all for making friends, but I'm not sure these new ones are going to last long," Bobby said to him after lunch. The tracking party remained manned, and sonar was looking for the proverbial needle in the South-China-Sea-haystack, but other than that, *Bluefish* steamed at condition III. Not being at battle stations with a Russian so close was exhausting.

"If the war returns, you're spot on." Alex grimaced. "Until then..."

"Yeah, but what if they find out about the war coming back to life before we do?"

"Then we dodge that missile-like torpedo of theirs and shoot them in the fucking face," Alex replied.

Bobby's jaw dropped. "Dodge it? You really think we could do that?"

Alex shrugged. "I've got a couple of ideas."

Executing those ideas in a *Cero*-class boat would be hard, but Alex didn't add that. First, because there was no evidence that their new Russian friend would turn on them; *Andromeda* lurked at the edges of their sonar range, trolling along in a search pattern mirroring *Bluefish's* about fifteen nautical miles to the northeast. Also, because undermining his crew's confidence was *stupid*. If they did get in a shootout with *Andromeda*, hesitation could be fatal. Better his crew think his ideas might be good than give them reason to doubt when the chips were down.

"You're serious."

"Yeah, but that's not the mission right now," he replied. "As much fun as it is to think about being shot at, we've still got a long and slow search ahead of us."

"And then we shoot at the end of that," Bobby said.

Alex nodded. "And then we shoot."

Hours crept by. Alex's crew was too experienced to turn this into what the navy called a "sweat-ex," or sweat exercise, meaning that everyone would spin right into a tizzy, missing sleep, food, and concentrating only on the hunt. Some of them—like Alex—had firsthand knowledge of just how hairy a long wartime engagement could be; that in turn meant everyone ate, slept, and relaxed when they weren't on watch. Alex didn't care if his sailors watched movies, played Spades and/or cribbage, or if they ate their brains with phone games, so long as they took a goddamned break.

He knew he'd need them sharp when the time came. Hell, he knew *he* needed to be at his best when they finally found the damned Chinese boomer...but forcing himself to relax was harder. In the end, it took watching a double marathon of westerns in the wardroom with Bobby, Lou, and various junior officers. That keyed Alex down long enough that he almost slept through the night.

Like everyone else, he spent breakfast trying to pretend his dreams hadn't been full of nuclear annihilation.

27 May 2040

What possessed her to make that offer? One day later, Katerina still didn't know. Was it tactically sound? Smart? That answer was obvious. Yet she had not expected to offer to work *with* Coleman instead of hurrying to beat him to the prize. Ambition remained one of her calling cards. Katerina Revnik was going to the top, and she was not going to let anything stop her.

Except, perhaps, good strategy. She still intended to find the *Jin*-class boomer, but in the case where she didn't...getting a piece of the kill was still a share of the glory. Besides, this guaranteed that *Bluefish* wouldn't crawl all over *Andromeda*, crowding them and making their hunt even harder. Now they could remain a respectable distance apart, maximizing the chances that *someone* would find the *Jin*. Yes, her country wanted—no, needed—to deny America the victory of killing those ULA madmen. But the true mission, the one that mattered, was stopping nuclear war.

Closing her eyes, Katerina leaned back against the bulkhead in her stateroom. She sat on her bed, legs crossed and shoes off. She'd wanted to meditate, but twenty minutes of trying told her she was not going to manage that. Perhaps it was the pressure. The feeling wiggled like ants under her skin, and Katerina was more *alive* than she'd ever been. Perhaps fate had been kind when it killed her gymnastic dreams. This was what she was made for.

Her phone buzzed, and she picked it up without opening her eyes. "This is the captain."

"This is Daniil," her second-in-command said. "We have received the official Chinese report on the taking of *Jianggezhuang* and the sinking of *Changzheng 7*. It is in your email."

"Thank you." Katerina smiled as Daniil hung up. Captain Third Rank Daniil Zhukov wasn't much of a talker; he said little and listened much. However, she knew that if Daniil called her about the report, it was worth reading.

In his customary fashion, the copy Daniil forwarded to Katerina was notated and the important parts were highlighted for her attention. Katerina appreciated that; she wasn't the biggest reader, preferring more visual mediums. She'd always been a woman of action, one who wanted to put her hands on things in order to learn. Her new love of comic books was unexpected, and she was self-aware enough to know her ego likely fed that fervor. After all, who could fail to adore a comic book heroine based on oneself?

Katerina was no academic, but with a second-in-command like Daniil, she didn't need to be. The sections he indicated as needing her attention flew by, right until she reached the section he'd noted was critical.

Changzheng 7 was on course 028, speed 6 knots when she detected Changzheng 18. *While closing with the target to acquire a firing solution,* Changzheng 7 *experienced an unreported fault in the port-side sonar array. This fault prevented detection of* Changzheng 14 *as she closed with* Changzheng 7 *from the east.*

Changzheng 14 was traveling at 15 knots, course unknown. The stolen attack submarine collided with Changzheng 7 midships on her port side. At time of collision, Changzheng 7 was at action stations, and her watertight doors were shut. This precaution saved some of the crew.

Changzheng 7 rolled three hundred and sixty degrees before righting herself; however, rampant flooding from the damage as well quickly caused the submarine to sink. Twenty-seven of the crew of one hundred survived and were picked up by the Taiwanese Navy. Changzheng 14 *appears to have escaped with minimal damage.*

Katerina's eyebrows shot up; there were pictures. The Chinese—she could not quite recall which one—must have had an aircraft right on top of *Changzheng 7* to snap pictures of the submarine as she went turtle on the surface. Seven or eight pictures were dedicated to the sinking submarine, and then a handful more were of the waterlogged crew struggling to swim. Katerina hoped that the photographer hadn't been on rescue duty; making submariners swim while snapping pictures was the kind of move she expected out of Americans.

"Lucky fools," Katerina breathed. There was nothing in the report indicating where *Changzheng 14* had gone, never mind the location of the real prize, *Changzheng 18*.

Damn those communists. Why did every submarine in the same class get the *same* annoying name with just a number attached? Telling them apart in the report gave her a headache. A quick online search told her that "*changzheng*" meant "long march," which was equally annoying to read over and over again. At least the Americans gave all of their ships and submarines different names. She could only imagine if every damned report read *Cero 893* versus *Cero 840* versus *Virginia 775*. She groaned and rubbed her eyes.

The report was dry, overly long, and boring, but it did tell her one critical thing: *Changzheng 14* would protect *Changzheng 18*. Katerina snarled a curse under her breath and corrected herself: the *Shang* would protect the *Jin*. Good. That was so much easier.

The *Shang*-class attack sub was still a guard dog. It was like the old Soviet doctrine: send an attack boat out to protect the missile submarine when it got underway. Simplistic, if generally effective...assuming the attack sub was willing and able to act.

This one clearly was.

Drumming her fingers against her desk, Katerina started running through scenarios in her mind. The *Shang* was willing to ram, was it? Perhaps she could distract it somehow. Or get it to ram *Bluefish*. She frowned. No, that was unworthy of her. They were not at war. *Bluefish* was an ally today. Perhaps she would be an enemy tomorrow, but first, they had to save the world, didn't they? It was time to put enmity aside.

She stared at the report for a few more minutes, ideas whirling through her head. Once she—or Coleman—found the boomer, what would happen? Would they both shoot and forget about the *Shang*? Or was it time to turn things on their head?

Now that was a thought.

"You know, I'd really like a way to talk to *Andromeda* without the whole world overhearing us," Alex said.

"Technically, it's only anyone in sonar range." Bobby stroked his chin as he lounged on the small couch in Alex's stateroom, his feet kicked up and head leaning against a discount store pillow. "That's about twenty to thirty nautical miles in these conditions."

"Show off."

Bobby laughed as he adjusted the pillow. It was maroon and gold, reminded Alex of his alma mater, and had cost about five bucks. If it went down with *Bluefish* and Alex didn't, he wouldn't shed many tears. Cheap and replaceable defined everything he'd brought on board. "It's only math, Captain," he replied. "I thought you liked math?"

"I very much do. I just dislike showoffs. Something ego something something." Alex grinned. "It's you extroverts."

"You know, it's not my fault that I was created in this good-looking, smart, and practically *sublime* form." Bobby waved both hands vaguely at his chest and then mimed fanning himself. "I'd be pretty intimidated, too."

Alex snorted. "If only your self-esteem was a weapon we could use on the enemy."

"Sir, my self-esteem is toxic. It'd poison everyone here before it got to the other side."

"That's a shame. I suppose I'll have to resort to ramming."

Bobby's laugh cut short as he turned to study Alex. "Hold on. That's not a joke."

"Not really, no." Alex grimaced. "I'm no fan of the idea, mind you. In fact, it's close to the bottom of my to-do list."

"Not even on your bingo card?"

"Oh, fuck no." He shook his head and glanced at the chart. "But if we run out of ways to shoot this cat, and that's the option we've got..."

"You know this isn't USS *Dallas*, right?" Bobby sat up straight, not noticing how the pillow went flying. "I'm going to pretend I didn't hear that idea until it's *way* too late to be terrified and just move back to the *totally* rational thing you said just five minutes ago. Why do you want to talk to *Andromeda*? I mean, we already talked to them. And it was weird. Way weird."

"You're telling me. I was part of that whackadoodle conversation." Alex's smile went crooked; he knew that no one wanted to hear that they might ram the boomer—and thus all die—so he let the change of subject slide without comment. "But it told us that Captain Revnik wants to work with us. That's as incredible as it is unexpected, but how the flying fuck are we supposed to pull that off?"

"Yeah, that's tough without getting in close and talking on a circuit everyone can overhear."

"Which makes close coordination impossible. And that, in turn, is a shitty-ass way to cause a blue-on-blue disaster," Alex replied.

"You sure it isn't blue-on-red?" Bobby asked. "I mean, I'm all for making friends, but I get the distinct feeling these friends aren't going to last."

"It's not the Cold War, Bobby." Calling Russia "the reds" had caught on again; before two years ago, Alex hadn't ever heard that outside of history books or film, but it was all over the internet.

It was stupid. The Russian flag *did* have red in it nowadays, but it was—ironically—red, white, and blue. With blue on top. This red-versus-blue nonsense felt like a goddamned video game. Of course his daughters loved it. One glimpse at his elder daughter's social media accounts showed that Bobbie actually posted *videos* about that crap...after which Alex learned his lesson and stayed very far away from anything either daughter posted online. He was a child of the digital age. He should've known better. But he was also a parent, which he supposed made him an idiot.

"Sure feels like. No one's shooting, everyone's tense, and now we're talking nuclear missiles."

"Point."

"Okay. You're trying to talk to the Russians. Like...talk. What about an email?" Bobby asked.

Alex blinked. "You think that they're like us and put emails on their boat's social media?"

"Odds are pretty good. They like to get fan mail to their sub captains. They even have a comic book based on Revnik."

"A *what?*" Alex's jaw dropped.

"Yeah, Lou speaks Russian. He showed me the comic last week. It's all over Russian-speaking stores." Bobby snickered. "Revnik looks hot."

"Jesus, Bobby." Alex had only seen one picture of his Russian counterpart; it was a cold and professional shot of the type that did no one any favors. Like most Russian officers, she didn't smile, instead wearing a stern expression that probably meant to intimidate.

"What? I'm single."

Alex shook his head. "Call your old roommate, then. And Weps. If we're going to do IT cartwheels, we should talk through the ramifications."

"You got it, sir." Bobby darted out of the room like a shot, leaving Alex to think in his wake.

Was this idea insane? Possibly. Did it risk breaching operational security? Certainly. OPSEC was pounded into every submariner's skill—these days, a security clearance was required just to be assigned to a crew—but tactical realities trumped the need to keep secrets. Or at least Alex thought so. No way would Commodore Banks approve.

Banks, however, was not here. Even if he'd give Alex a goddamned earful for this if he found out, it wasn't Banks who had the duty and responsibility of destroying this rogue Chinese boomer. If Alex didn't use every tool at his disposal and he failed, the world would pay the price. Alex swallowed. He didn't like carrying the weight of the world on his shoulders. Responsibility, even being the navy's go-to submarine captain, wasn't new, but this? This was insane.

Yet he was the one in the seat. He'd accepted this mission. Now it was up to him to get the job done.

Drumming his fingers against his desk, Alex pulled up a blank email and started drafting what he'd say to Captain Revnik, assuming they had the chance to talk. He wouldn't betray national secrets. Not a chance. But how to put together a coherent plan of cooperation when they were limited to one or two emails? Probably one. Anything more would make the guys and gals in IT shit themselves.

By the time he had a rough draft, Bobby returned with Rose and Lou.

"Rene has the watch," Rose said as she perched on the couch next to Bobby. Lou took the second chair after closing the door, making the narrow stateroom feel even more cramped.

Such was the joy of naval service. At least this boat didn't have holes in the carpet.

"Thanks." Alex always appreciated it when his folks answered questions before he could ask them. "Bobby tell you two what's up?"

"Yeah." Rose scrunched up her face. "Smells a little like treason, to be honest, even if it technically isn't. Gives me the fucking willies."

Lou shrugged before speaking in his usual Southern drawl. "I'm all for giving peace a go, Captain."

"Personally, I'm all for stopping the lunatics who now possess nuclear weapons," Alex said. "Anyone has a better idea, I'm all ears."

"Fuck, I wish," Rose replied.

"What she said." Bobby jerked a thumb at Rose, his old friend from the Academy. She'd missed a semester due to sickness, but they'd been as thick as thieves until Alex upended things by asking for Bobby to be his XO. They were still good friends, but they managed to mostly balance that with professionalism while on board the boat. In peacetime, one or the other would've been transferred. The navy disliked even the *appearance* of fraternization, even when the pair in question considered themselves bas-ackwards siblings and had no romantic inclinations. However, war changed a lot of rules.

"A little birdie tells me that you speak Russian." Alex turned to Lou.

"I read it better than I speak it, Captain, but I'm conversational if you need someone," Lou replied.

"Dare I ask why?"

Lou shrugged. "There was a Russian girl in my class in high school. We dated, I learned more from her, and then I got a ticket to the Defense Language Institute when I was enlisted. I started as an IS, you know."

Alex felt his eyebrows shoot up. "You started in intel? Damn. What made you cross-rate to engineering?"

"Downsizing. You know how it is. Being a nuclear machinists' mate was job security, I was still a kid, I already liked subs, and my high school jobs had all been working for mechanics. The navy wasn't going to say no."

Shit, those three sentences told Alex more about his engineer's past than the past year and a half. Yeah, he knew about Lou's drama queen of ex-wife and no kids, and he knew what kind of movies and books Lou liked as well as the wicked sense of humor that slipped out when he was drunk. But Lou was generally quiet and laid back, which meant he didn't volunteer much.

"Well, I'd say the navy won. You keep up with that Russian?" he asked.

"I didn't before the war, but it seemed like a good idea when the shooting started," Lou drawled. "I got the ITs to put a copy of Rosetta Stone on the network and went to town." He nodded at Bobby. "That's why he knows. I did my homework in the stateroom."

"Well, then, your mission is simple. Take a look at all of the *Andromeda* social media you can find, and try to find me an email address someone will answer. Preferably Captain Revnik."

"Not a problem, Captain. It shouldn't be too hard."

"Thanks." Alex glanced at Rose. "You want to work with the IT men to make sure that there's no block on the network that'll stop that email? I know radio belongs to the navigator, but we're rather lacking one at the moment, and Bobby's going to be busy helping me not step on my dick with this email."

"Better him than me." Rose's smile was fleeting. "I'll go check, sir. And I'll bully them into pulling down whatever firewall we've got."

"Thank you. All of you." Alex sucked in a deep breath. "Let's get to work."

Chapter 8

Compatriots

28 May 2040, the South China Sea

The email came in before Katerina even headed to breakfast. She was an early riser and liked to work out before eating; that morning, she hopped off the treadmill, took a shower, and plopped down in front of the computer as she dried her hair. Important emails came at all hours, particularly when her boat was seven hours ahead of Moscow time. She didn't expect much in the way of intelligence or an orders change, but it was still worth checking.

She did not expect an email from the address co@ssn843.navy.mil.

Blinking, Katerina dropped her hair towel and opened the email. She knew *Bluefish's* hull number; having been sunk by the all-too-average *Cero*-class boat meant she'd looked up everything about *Bluefish*. Her disappointment over the boat being just another *Cero*—not even one of the Improved boats!—still stung from time to time, but excitement pushed it aside today. She was certain that no one told Captain Coleman to email her. The man was unorthodox to a fault, which meant this would be, at the very least, interesting.

Fortunately, her English was good, because she doubted her counterpart spoke Russian.

Captain Revnik,

I apologize for emailing you out of the blue, but this seemed like a less likely way to be overheard than closing the range for another Gertrude call. Given the recent state of war between our nations, formal information sharing is obviously out of the question. I don't believe our systems are compatible, anyway, so any attempt to send you track data would result in sending electrons into the ocean for no reason.

That said, I think a little more coordination is in order. Our Chinese liaison informed us that his submarine—Changzheng 7—was sunk when the rogue attack sub rammed them. The condition of the other boat is unknown, but I think we have to assume it's still combat capable. I think we also have to assume it's willing to resort to the same tactics. We also don't know enough about this Undersea Liberation Army to know what brand of fanatics they are or aren't, so I intend to take that threat seriously.

Same with their threat to launch missiles. Our liaison says that his government—which one he did not say, though he seems to lean away from the communists—believes that the ULA can't have the launch codes. But our report of how the ULA took over Submarine Base Number 1 *and* successfully stole three submarines indicates that they have someone on the inside. How far inside, I don't know. I know it's a risk I'm not willing to take.

One of us may have to draw the Shang off so the other can shoot the boomer. I think that will come down to which one of us is closer; if we shoot at the attack sub without locating the boomer, I fear that will only encourage the boomer to launch.

I propose we continue our search patterns. Whichever contact we find to the north will belong to you; Bluefish will prosecute the southern one. Whoever finds the attack boat should maneuver in a way that allows detection at a range further than their torpedoes can fire.

> *If our intel is correct, the Chinese Yu-6 torpedo is supposed to be a clone of our old Mark 48. That means its top speed is around 55 knots. I assume your* Pictor *is faster than that. Range should be about 15 nautical miles, perhaps less at top speed. We don't have solid reports on what a Type 093A can do in terms of speed, but it's safest to assume they can keep up if either of us sprints.*
>
> *Allowing the* Shang *to detect either one of us is probably the only way to draw them away from the boomer without missiles being fired. I think we must assume that the boomer will fire if they or their escort is threatened. Assuming that is certainly safer than the alternative.*
>
> *V/R,*
> *Captain Alex Coleman*
> *CO SSN 843*

Whistling, Katerina leaned back in her chair. That email was much, *much* bigger than her proposing their two submarines cooperate. In fact, she was fairly sure she'd broken at least one law by reading it. Or had she? Did an armistice repeal Russia's wartime laws? She was no legal scholar; Katerina didn't even want to guess.

Instead, she cracked her knuckles and started typing her response. Coleman was right. This was not an opportunity they could afford to pass up. Not if either of them wanted to survive and meet their grandchildren.

She was almost finished when her phone rang. "This is the captain."

"Good morning, Captain. I think you might want to come to the attack center," Daniil said. "We have a contact at medium range, moving southeast at nine knots. Initial analysis indicates a Type 093 *Shang*-class submarine."

Katerina's heart dropped to her feet, but she replied calmly: "I will be up momentarily."

Turning back to the computer, Katerina finished up the email with three more sentences and clicked send without looking back.

She had a rebel submarine to find and sink.

The Strait of Malacca

"This has got to be the *worst* fucking piece of water to listen to sonar in," Sonar Technician (Submarines) Third Class Boyer muttered. "You couldn't hear a whale dying here."

"There, there, Boyer," Wilson said from where he stood behind the manned sonar consoles. He was training Boyer as sonar supervisor today, which meant he didn't get a cushy seat or console, but he had his headset plugged into a spare hookup and was listening with one ear. "I'll have you know that whales die too quietly to pick them out, even in friendly pieces of water."

Boyer, a late-twenties sonar operator who *should've* made second class years ago, scowled. The expression only highlighted his red freckles and made his balding more obvious. "Fine, it's too loud to hear if we run *over* another goddamned submarine, let alone a Chinese boomer that doesn't want to be found. None of the filters work for shit."

"That's because you're autotuning. Places like this, you've got to manually blank out the frequencies you don't want. You can tell the computer all day what you're looking for, but it's still going to be a stupid computer. Whoever wrote these programs was a chump. Garbage in, garbage out."

Boyer snickered, then craned his head back to look at Wilson. "You think we'll find them?"

"I know that if we do, the captain's going to be quick as fuck off the trigger." Wilson shrugged. "They probably haven't made it this far yet. Why leave the muddy brown waters around China if they're threatening to nuke Chinese targets?"

"Cause ballistic missiles have terrifyingly long ranges?" STS2 Zins—who was already sonar sup qualified—said from Boyer's left.

Wilson shivered. He didn't like thinking about Armageddon, not even the old movie that was so bad it was good. "There is that."

An uncomfortable silence fell as the three contemplated the end of the world. Wasn't that the happiest? If he hadn't already gone sober, it might've been enough to scare Wilson straight.

Fuck, maybe he'd get drunk. Who cared if the world was going to end? His meager attempts at salvaging his career wouldn't matter in a nuclear apocalypse. If he survived, the only thing anyone would care about in that situation was his ability to work sonar like magic.

Wilson could do that drunk. He was pretty sure, anyway.

"Sonar, what's the range to that French destroyer?" Commander Kennedy asked, making Wilson jump.

"Thirty-two thousand yards and change, sir," Zins replied before Wilson calmed his racing heart.

That was in range, wasn't it? Wilson wasn't a torpedoman, but he liked memorizing facts, and the Mark 84 ASV had a maximum range of twenty-one nautical miles, or forty-two thousand yards. This wouldn't be a great shot, but *Kansas* could make it work against a surface ship. French destroyers were nasty customers, for all the frogs called them frigates, but they weren't that fast. Surface ships with old-fashioned screws tended not to be. Those suckers could only spin so fast.

"Get me a solution, fire control," Kennedy ordered.

Wilson blinked. That was a *touch* better than jumping straight to inputting that solution straight into the torpedoes' brains like they usually did, but...

"Aren't we at peace?" Boyer whispered.

"Mind your console," Wilson said, mostly to shut the idiot up before the captain overheard.

Kennedy wasn't the kind of captain who was open to other opinions, not unless the talker mirrored Kennedy's own ideas back at him. Lieutenant Commander Song, their XO, was famous for that, but neither Wilson nor his team were exactly Kennedy's type.

Oh. Ew. That brought up mental images of the captain and the XO in bed together, and Wilson *did fucking not* want to imagine that. In fact—

"Captain, we just got a FLASH message," Song said, intruding on Wilson's extra gross and inadvertent daydream.

"What now?" Kennedy crossed his arms as Wilson peeked over his shoulder, looking like the same petulant child he'd been ever since he was told to mind the back door here in the SOM instead of doing the sexy shit like hunting those rogue Chinese boats down. "If they fired, it would be a Pinnacle NUCFLASH."

"They have not fired," Song said without looking up from the message tablet. "But the Undersea Liberation Army has said, I quote, 'Our demands have not been met despite giving governments of China a generous amount of time. If the various governments of China do not surrender within twenty-four hours, the Undersea Liberation Army's missile submarine will launch nuclear missiles at Beijing, Shanghai, and Taipei.'"

"What the fuck?" Kennedy snarled. "And we're out all the way the fuck out here?!"

"There is no news on the location of the missile submarine, sir," Song said. For once, she sounded cautious, like she didn't know how to manage Kennedy's temper today.

"You can sure fucking bet they won't fire from here. They'd be too afraid of someone shooting the goddamned missiles down." Kennedy slapped the horizontal screen of the nav table. "There's so many warships in the SOM that you could goddamned walk to Singapore without touching water."

The way Song's face twitched said that she wanted to call him on that *extreme* exaggeration, but she didn't. Not before Kennedy continued, anyway:

"Nav, get me a time-distance to the south tip of the South China Sea. Sprinting," Kennedy ordered.

"Nav, aye." Lieutenant Grippo's voice was so flat it could've served as a surfboard, but that was nothing new. Grippo was Kennedy's favorite target, and he just *loved* picking on her.

"He's not seriously thinking of sprinting around down here, is he?" Boyer whispered. "We'll run up someone's stern like *Hartford* did *New Orleans.*"

Bud couldn't argue with Boyer's logic; that accident might've taken place thirty years ago, but it cost the navy over $120 million dollars to repair both ships and the sub school still used it as a case study. Still, now wasn't the time. Not with the captain in another fucking temper.

"Put your headset on and keep your eyes on your console if you're worried about hitting shit," he hissed.

"Sorry." Boyer cringed and returned his attention to his screen. Zins shot Wilson a raised eyebrow look, however, and all he could do was shrug.

No one else in control was saying anything, that was for sure. The silence was heavier than usual, particularly with Kennedy pacing and grumbling about *how fucking long it took to get work done around here.* Yeah. Wilson wished he could sit at a goddamned console and pretend to be fascinated, too, but the third sonar console was tagged out for repairs.

"Sir, we'd need more than a day to get there." Grippo's voice was quiet, but in the eerie stillness, it might as well have been a firecracker.

"Of fucking course it will. XO, check that time-distance."

"I already did, sir. The navigator is correct," Song replied.

Kennedy's string of swear words impressed even Wilson.

"Conn, Sonar, new track bearing three-four-five, range forty thousand yards," Chief Andreas reported thirty seconds after Alex wandered into control after breakfast, his mind still whirling with the Undersea Liberation Army's demands. Would they really fire? He couldn't afford to assume otherwise. What if they didn't find the boomer? What if no one did?

To say his heart was in his throat would be the understatement of a relatively new century. Fortunately, Chief Andreas gave him a whole different type of nerds. "Tonals match a *Jin*-class submarine."

"Sonar, Conn, is it the *right* one?" Rose had the watch, and her voice was sharp; a chill ran down Alex's spine as he considered how disastrous shooting the *wrong* Chinese missile sub would be. That could be worse than missing the right one.

Then again, if the three Chinese governments—or the two that owned *Jins*, anyway—had any sense, they'd have pulled all their missile boats into port. But had they? Alex turned to Commander Liao Fan.

"Do you have confirmation that your governments have recalled all their boomers?" he asked.

Liao hesitated. "I believe so. There were not many missile submarines underway when *Fourteen* was captured. But there are…communications issues when two governments each claim a submarine." He grimaced. "The orders were sent, but I cannot guarantee that all captains have obeyed the orders."

"Well, isn't that a beautiful fucking travesty?" Alex bit back a groan. "Any particular way to identify *Fourteen*? Neither of your government sent a sonar profile along."

"Those are closely guarded." Liao fidgeted. "However, my sonar operator said that there is some sort of 'bump of sound' on the sixty-five hertz line. Is that enough?"

"Let's pass it to Chief Andreas and find out."

Chief Andreas, *Bluefish's* senior sonar operator, seemed a bit dubious when called to control to learn that factoid, but she headed back to sonar to share it with her team. Minutes ticked by as *Bluefish* crept every closer to the *Jin*-class boat. The boomer made things easier as she drifted forward at just three knots, not keeping much of a course so much as wandering around.

Were they doing "box ops?" Alex scratched his chin. Doing box operations just meant tooling around in the same patch of water until an assignment or target arrived…but it also could be a *launch* box, which put a sub in the optimal position to fire on their designated targets.

"How much does the ULA know about submarines?" Alex asked. "Their messages make it obvious they're fanatics, but are they fanatics who can drive and fight a sub?"

Liao frowned. "We assumed that they kept some of the crews on board and are forcing them to operate the submarine."

"Shit, that would suck." It also meant he was going against *some* trained professionals...but how many? What percentage? Liao was clearly uncomfortable with the idea, particularly since they all knew this would end with shooting, but Alex didn't get a chance to ask for more details because Chief Andreas's voice echoed out of the speaker to his right.

"Conn, Sonar, track 6222 has a weird bump on the sixty-five hertz line. Confirmed as *Changzheng 14* and marked as hostile. New track number 7222."

Alex's heart did a backflip. "Conn, aye." He turned to look at his team. "It's showtime. OOD, take us to battle stations and close with the enemy. Stay below ten knots."

"Battle stations, OOD, aye." Rose turned to the chief of the watch. "Chief of the Watch, pass the word to set battle stations torpedo. Silently."

"Chief of the Watch, aye."

Alex did not watch as the word was passed throughout the boat, with messengers going to berthing and out of the way spaces to ensure his sailors were awake and ready without the benefit of the general alarm. Setting battle stations *silently* meant not slamming hatches, passing the word on the 1MC, and basically trying to make like a hole in the water.

Bluefish's sailors were good at this. Alex didn't need to micromanage. Nor did he need to tell Rose what course to steer. She knew her business and would get the boat where she needed to be.

Within a minute, Bobby O'Kane arrived to stand by Alex's side. "We find them?" Bobby asked.

"We've found the boomer. No sign of *Eighteen* yet."

"So we're still in danger of playing bumper cars but not getting any tickets to redeem for prizes. Great." Bobby's smile was a little too big. "It's kind of like the *Blues Brothers*. Every chase they got into involved smashing up cars. We're just bigger."

"You're a font of optimism today, aren't you?" Alex chuckled.

"I'll get optimistic again once someone sinks that *Shang* before it can ram us. *Bluefish* just got new tiles and a nice paintjob. Anyone ruins that and I'll go postal," Bobby replied.

"You hear that, Weps? Don't scratch the paint," Alex said. "XO will pout."

"I said postal, not pout," Bobby objected as Rose laughed.

"I heard you." Alex grinned. "You ready to take this puppy down?"

"I like puppies a lot more than missile boats, so not if it's an actual puppy," Bobby replied. "But if it's a boomer masquerading as a cute puppo, I'm in." He finished studying the chart. "I'm good to take the deck, Rose."

"All yours." Rose raised her voice. "Attention in control. This is Weps. The XO has the deck."

"This is the XO, I have the deck and the conn," Bobby said.

Taking a deep breath, Alex grabbed the handset for the 1MC, the boat's general announcing system. Talking on it was a risk—any noise was—but he felt like his crew needed to know what was going on.

"*Bluefish*, this is the captain," he said as a cold chill ran through his body from the top of his head to somewhere near his ankles. "We're closing with the Chinese boomer now. You all know the stakes. You know the ULA has threatened to fire today. While we aren't at war, the world is at stake...and we'll probably have one chance at this. That means we have to do everything—and anything—we can to stop this rogue missile sub from firing. Whatever it takes, we'll do it."

Alex paused to glance around control, acutely aware of how every eye in the space was fastened on him. Pushing his old fear of public speaking down took a gargantuan effort, but he continued: "We've been together a while now. We've done the impossible. But now I must ask you to do the impossible one more time, because if we don't, there may be no second chances."

Should he say he was prepared to ram the boomer? No, worrying his crew like that was foolish. Any distraction could be fatal, and that would be one *big* honking distraction.

"I know you'll all do your best," he said instead of opening that can of toxic worms. "Thank you all."

Hanging up the mic before he made an ass out of himself was old habit by now. Ignoring Bobby's shit-eating grin was harder.

"You're getting better," Bobby said.

Alex mock scowled at him. "When the hell did you get so uppity?"

"I don't know." Bobby shrugged. "*Someone* asked for me to be his XO and arranged a whole promotion and everything. I can't imagine who would be that stupid."

"Me, neither. Someone should tell that guy to pound sand."

Bobby's laughing response was cut off by the radio watch calling in via the intercom box. "Captain, Radio, you wanted to be alerted if you got an email from *Andromeda*."

"Radio, Captain, send it to the message tablet and bring it on in."

"Radio, aye."

Less than a minute passed before the radio watch arrived in control, handed Alex the message traffic tablet, and retreated back to their quiet and dark closet. Alex didn't watch the petty officer go; instead, he pulled up that email and skimmed it.

"Anything fun?" Bobby asked.

"Revnik says she's on the *Shang's* tail. She also agrees to my proposal."

Bobby's eyebrows wagged like they belonged on a cartoon character. "Gee, Captain, you might want to tell wife before you go *that* far."

"Hey, some of us think that's a great idea," Rose cut in from the weapons corner. "You're not the only one who thinks she's hot, XO. Maybe the other Captain Coleman agrees."

Alex laughed so hard his sides hurt. "She might," he said. "I haven't asked."

Nancy had dated a girl between their sophomore year breakup and getting back together. At one point, Alex thought she might be into her roommate, but they were more like sisters. His wife's interests had never bothered him; Nancy liked to say that she had twice as many choices and she still chose him, which *still* made Alex feel warm inside, even after more than two decades together.

"Well, if you're going to start a polycule, count me out," Bobby said. "I'm not opposed to the idea, at least not with women, but I draw the line at dudes. And double line at my captain. Sorry, sir, you're just not my type."

"What happened to 'it's not gay if you're underway'?" Rose asked.

"That's just your life, Rosie. Don't dress it up."

Alex gave folks a few moments to laugh before raising his voice. "All right, settle down. We can have fun again after we stop these assholes." He turned back to the bitch box. "Sonar, Conn, what's our range to the boomer?"

"Conn, Sonar, about thirty-seven thousand yards."

"Conn, aye." Alex took a deep breath. The Mark 84 ASV, or Advanced Spearfish Variant, had a maximum effective range of about twenty-one nautical miles, or forty-two thousand yards. That meant they'd been in range of the boomer from the moment *Bluefish* detected her; however, the ASV wasn't the fastest torpedo in the world at eighty-seven knots. Shooting at long range gave the enemy time to dodge.

Not to mention time to fire.

Alex did some quick math. At their current range, a torpedo would need about twelve-and-a-half minutes to get to the target. Could they spin up a missile that fast? Didn't matter. No way was he taking that chance.

"Sonar, Conn, are they below the layer or above it?" he asked. "Any maneuvering?"

"Negative. They're tooling along fat, dumb, and happy on the same course. Their depth is about three hundred feet above the layer."

"We speculated that the ULA 'crew' does not know much about submarines," Liao said from where he was squeezed in between two consoles, obviously trying to stay out of the way. "We are not sure, however, if they have any of the original crew on board to help them."

"You think the boat's actual crew would help them launch a missile?"

Liao grimaced. "I think they might be forced into helping. There's no knowing what the terrorists will do to them."

"Good point." It wasn't one Alex wanted to think about, but he needed to play this smart. The possibility of trained submariners on the other end complicated things immensely. "Their choice of ramming indicates they might not know how to fire a torpedo...or have the access to do so. You lock your firing tubes during peacetime?"

"Yes. They also might not have torpedoes on board," Liao replied. "We only had a handful of—what do you call them, warshots?—non-exercise torpedoes on *Seven*. *Fourteen* was not planned to get underway soon, and we have a torpedo shortage."

"Yeah?" Alex's eyebrows shot up.

Liao nodded. "No one is sure which government they should requisition weapons from, but neither is sending them."

"That sounds like a rodeo I *don't* want to be part of," Bobby said.

"Quite."

"All right," Alex said. "We operate on the assumption that there are at least some professionals over there. They might not be calling the shots, but we can't afford to be careless. Let's plan accordingly."

"How are you feeling about their threat to fire?" Bobby asked.

"Like trash dipped in dogshit. We should be able to hear when they go shallow and flood tubes, but I'm not a fan of how long it's going to take us to get into range," Alex replied. "At this speed, it's going to take us more than an hour to get into our preferred firing range."

Bobby made a face. "That feels like asking for trouble."

"Yeah, but if we fired a torp from here, they'd have about twelve minutes to shoot. A good American crew can empty their missile tubes in that time."

Alex didn't need to look around to see the pale faces. He could feel the creep of terror crawling up his spine as one moment after another passed. Decision paralysis could kill them as surely as making a mistake, but the pressure was higher than even Alex was used to.

Convoy 57 hadn't been this bad. There'd barely been time to think of the danger that day, and even with thousands of civilian lives on the line, well, that didn't compare to what even one ballistic missile could do to the world. His heart wanted to do worse than race; Alex swore he could feel it skipping beats and then throwing in makeup ones every couple seconds. How the *hell* was he supposed to pull this off from stealth?

"Our best silent speed is twenty-eight knots." Bobby paused his pacing to play with a grease pencil, rolling it between his fingers. "You want to kick it up a bit?"

"Yeah, let's come up to eighteen knots." Alex still felt being conservative was safer. Detection coming too early would give the boomer a chance to fire. But even this increase cut his time to close with the enemy by a half hour.

Fifty-two minutes and change was still too long. Only one of those minutes passed as Bobby brought the boat up in speed; this slow, *Bluefish* barely even trembled.

"Sonar, Captain, let me know the moment the target changes depth or opens missile hatches."

"Sonar, aye."

Rose looked up from the weapons control console. "You think they might be dumb enough to open hatches from five hundred feet?"

"Only if we're lucky."

"If I was some pissed-off Chinese sailor who had my sub stolen...I'd tell them they could do it from there, damn the consequences," Rose replied. "It could kill them, but at least they wouldn't destroy the world. And they've *got* to know that opening those hatches is one of the most unique sounds in the sonar world. Sonar from around the planet will pick that up, and then *everyone* will want to drop a missile on their heads."

"Not everyone finds self-sacrifice that easy," Master Chief Ginger Baker said. The chief of the boat, or COB, stood at her station behind the helm and lee helm—sometimes called pilot and co-pilot—consoles, looking pensive.

"When it's you or the world, you should get with the goddamned program," Rose said. "Not you, COB. Generic you."

Baker's smile was thin. "I got that, thanks, Weps. But I was thinking of *who* those ULA people kept alive. They probably killed the officers and senior enlisted and just kept the technical experts—or someone technical *enough*—alive. If I was going to steal a submarine plus some crew, I'd make sure the people most likely to lead a mutiny against me were dead and gone already. Anyone left will be less brave."

"I don't like admitting you're right," Rose said, her nose crinkling. "Fuck."

"Same." Baker shrugged. "Not much to do about it other than be ready, though."

Being ready was literally the definition of Alex's job, but all he could do right now was wipe his sweaty palms on the legs of his coveralls and force himself to wait.

"This game sucks." He dug a hard candy out of his pocket and popped it in his mouth. "We've got to change the rules."

"What, you don't like the old-school stalk and approach, Captain?" Baker's eyebrows wagged.

"I like it a lot better in exercises." Alex rubbed the back of his sore neck, hoping the pain was only from stress. "Not when the fate of the goddamned world is at stake. What are our options?"

"Speed up to twenty-eight knots? The chance of detection is still pretty low, particularly if there aren't that many pros over there, like Master Chief says," Bobby said. "That would let us hit ten thousand yards in...thirty-four minutes. Ish."

"Assuming they maintain course and speed," Rose put in. "They could ruin our goddamned day by speeding up. And then we have nothing in reserve other than getting heard."

Bobby shrugged. "Okay, call it twenty-six knots. That extends intercept by about three minutes. No biggie."

"The other option is hauling ass and closing as fast as possible," Baker said. "At flank, we'd be at ten thousand yards in sixteen minutes. And we *could* fire earlier, just to keep them busy."

"Normally, I'd love that option, but this blue bitch of ours only has four tubes. If that *Shang* sneaks up on us while we're sprinting, we wouldn't be able to reload fast enough to shoot them both." Alex leaned against the chart table. How could he be so goddamned tired when adrenaline was racing through his system like crack?

"Would one torpedo keep them busy enough?" Bobby asked. "If it's amateur hour over there, one torpedo gets a lot scarier. No one likes getting shot at. We can all attest to that."

"Conn, Sonar, new contact! Track 7223, tonals resemble a *Shang*-class attack sub. Range is fifty-three thousand yards, bearing zero-one-niner. Her course and speed match the boomer."

"Conn, aye, break, look for a *Pictor* in her wake, please."

A tense moment passed before Chief Andreas replied: "Faint contact astern of the *Shang*. Computer cannot identify; they're beneath the layer."

"That would be Revnik." Calling Katerina Revnik by her name made her feel like an ally; was that a mindset Alex could afford?

Yeah. Today he could. Maybe things would change tomorrow.

"Sonar, Conn, what's the range from the *Shang* to the *Pictor*?" Bobby asked.

"About twenty thousand yards," Andreas replied.

"Conn, aye." Bobby twisted to look at Alex. "Looks like she's in closer than we are."

"Yeah, but if she fires before we do, the gig is up." Alex wished he'd thought to tell Revnik that in his email, but there wasn't time, not now. She'd be consumed by the tactical situation and not checking email.

Nor should he be *sending* one right about now. Any emissions increased the detection risk, no matter how trivial. Alex was old school in that one regard; he wanted his boat to be silent in tactical situations. He had no idea if Revnik agreed, and he didn't plan on finding out. The only concession he made to modern technology was keeping the comms wire out, which was *not* his normal M.O. But in this situation, receiving messages on time could change the tactical picture.

"Does she know that?" Bobby asked quietly, echoing his thoughts.

"I fucking hope so." Alex sighed. "She's good. We've got to trust that."

"Trusting a Russian still feels like wandering along a public street naked, but I agree that we don't have a choice."

"Yep."

Alex scratched his chin and considered his options. Sprinting would likely result in the boomer firing. The *Shang* wasn't in their own range yet—not if intel was right and the Yu-6 was a CBASS clone, making her range about thirty thousand yards—but they'd put down the pedal if *Bluefish* did. Even worse, the boomer might do the same, and while *Bluefish* was a lot faster than the boomer, anything could happen once the monkeys escaped the barrel. Combat was like that.

No, the slow-and-steady approach was the right one. He was sure of it. Alex ordered an increase in speed to twenty-six knots, however. Bobby was right. The chance of detection was very small under their best silent speed, and closing the range was imperative...even if he had to do so with caution.

Then why did his instincts tell him something was off?

Shaking his head, Alex pushed the feeling aside and concentrated on the enemy. Fifty minutes to go until firing range.

Chapter 9

Ride the Storm

About ten minutes of boredom later, circumstance made the decision for Alex.

"Conn, Sonar, I've got hull popping noises! She's going shallow!" Chief Andreas's voice rose with each syllable, and control went so quiet it was like everyone stopped breathing.

"All ahead flank!" Alex snapped. They were still too far away; ten nautical miles was inside the Mark 84's range, but reliability dropped against sophisticated opponents. Was the *Jin* good enough to dodge? Alex only had four torpedo tubes and didn't dare miss. "Weps, make all tubes ready in all respects, including opening the outer doors."

"Make all tubes ready in all respects, including opening the outer doors, Weps, aye," Rose replied crisply. "Target the boomer with all four?"

"Affirm."

Bluefish trembled as the sailor at the lee helm jammed the throttles forward. Alex, meanwhile, did math.

Fifty-seven knots was *Bluefish's* top speed. Maybe a hair more if they were lucky; Lou knew his shit and would do everything he could, short of endangering the reactor. Their torpedoes were thirty knots faster. At flank speed, *Bluefish* needed almost six minutes to get to ten thousand yards, where the hit probability for a Mark 84 ASV against a modern submarine increased to around sixty percent. Keeping the fish on the wire—with a human guiding it all the way to the target—increased the hit probability to a shocking ninety-five percent, but Alex couldn't reload with a torpedo on the wire.

Did he dare depend on four torpedoes to do the job? At this range, they'd need seven minutes to get to the target. By then, *Bluefish* would be at her preferred range and able to fire another salvo of torpedoes. His crew could reload in far less than five minutes if he cut the wires right away. Besides, Alex had twenty-six fish on board, and he would be happy to fire every last one of them in exchange for sinking this target.

Fish or cut bait? This wasn't the first time he'd had to make this decision, but the stakes had never been higher.

"Solution ready!" Rose said.

"Ship ready." Bobby spoke so fast his words almost overlapped hers.

"Tubes one through four, *fire*!" Alex's heart stuttered, but his voice remained steady. Thank God for experience.

"Conn, Sonar, four fish running hot, straight, and normal," STS2 Walkman reported.

"Conn, aye." Alex could feel his palms sweating and jammed his hands in his pockets to hide his nerves.

"Conn, Sonar, track 7223, *Shang* has increased speed and has turned to a new course. Speed approximately four-zero knots. Jane's says that's likely flank for them," Chief Andreas said before Alex could move away from the bitch box.

"Range?" Alex asked.

"About forty-one thousand yards."

"Conn, aye. Let me know if they speed up." Alex knew the Yu-6 torpedo had a range of about twenty-one nautical miles. The *Shang* was close enough to shoot...but probably not close enough to hit *Bluefish*. Alex couldn't spare those particular terrorists any attention.

They would just have to hope Revnik was quick enough on the trigger to get the *Shang* before the ULA attack boat could shoot *Bluefish*. And even if she wasn't... Alex swallowed. There were worse ways to die than saving the world.

Decision time.

"Cut the wires on tubes one and two, close the outer doors, and reload," Alex said. Splitting the difference felt cowardly, but his options were limited. "XO, keep us CBDR with the *Jin.*"

"Cut the wires, close the outer doors and reload, tubes one and two, Weps, aye!"

Bobby arched an eyebrow after he adjusted the boat's course. "You thinking something tricky, Captain?"

"More like the opposite. We're going to fire as soon as tubes one and two are reloaded, and we're going to sprint like hell on the heels of our torps. We'll keep firing until we sink her."

Or until we ram her, Alex didn't add. Bobby was smart, and the way his eyes went wide said the XO knew *exactly* what Alex was thinking.

Bobby nodded, met Alex's gaze...and said nothing.

"Conn, Sonar, torpedo in the water! *Two* torpedoes in the water, bearing zero-three-six, not inbound own ship!" STS2 Walkman's voice hit a fever pitch. "Torpedo speed...two hundred-plus knots? Torpedoes inbound *Shang.*"

"And that would be our friend." Alex felt a tense smile crease his face.

"She's got some serious juice over there." Bobby huffed. "Wish we could get some of that."

"That *Shkval* might seem sexy, but it's short ranged. She can't get the *Jin* from that far back." And Alex couldn't bet on *Andromeda* having any of the older Russian *Futlyar* torpedoes on board, either. Those were longer ranged, but they probably still didn't have enough legs to catch the boomer if she started running. He leaned toward the speaker. "Sonar, Conn, range to *Andromeda?*"

"Fifty-seven thousand yards. They're fifteen thousand yards behind the *Shang.*"

And the *Shang* was sprinting with all she had toward the boomer...and *Bluefish*. Would she change course with those hell torpedoes on her heels?

"Conn, aye." Alex looked up. The *Shang* was not his problem. "Time to reload, Weps?"

"Two mikes."

A glance at the plot told Alex that they were still about fifteen thousand yards from the boomer...and the boomer was maneuvering. His chest went tight. Surprise was out the window; now he had to be aggressive.

"Sonar, Conn, what the hell is the boomer doing?"

"She's turned her ass to us, still slow... Standby." A tense moment of silence passed before Chief Andreas continued; Alex barely dared breathe. "Missile hatches open! Tubes flooding!"

"Holy fuck," Alex whispered. "Those assholes are prepared to die to get nukes off?" He swallowed. "Chief Ree, you have those torps dialed in?"

"Straight to hell, sir," the fire control chief replied. He was driving both torpedoes himself instead of letting a junior sailor do so, his knuckles white on the controls.

"Weps, expedite that reloading. We don't have much time here." He glanced at Master Chief Baker. "How long does it take one of ours to go from flooding their tubes to missile away?"

The chief of the boat made a vague gesture with one hand. "We've never done it under fire, obviously, but the best time my crew on *Maine* ever did it was about three-and-a-half minutes. I'd guess that these guys will need at least twice that, unless they have the original missile crew on board."

"That's unlikely," Liao said from his corner, his voice so quiet that Alex had a hard time hearing it over the booming beat of his heart. "Initial reports from Jianggezhuang indicated that at least half the crew was left ashore."

"I'm not sure I want to roll that dice." Alex tried for a steadying deep breath, but it just made him more antsy.

Again, his eyes flicked back to the plot. Time felt sluggish, almost like slow motion, but Alex knew that was a lie borne of adrenaline. *Bluefish* continued to close the boomer at fifty-seven knots as the tension in her control room grew thicker and thicker. Alex wouldn't have said the walls were closing in, but damn, the space was starting to feel smaller. Meanwhile, her torpedoes, now about twenty-eight hundred yards ahead of her, continued at eighty-seven knots. Six minutes until impact.

No follow-on torpedo would get there faster, but Alex still planned on shooting everything he had. *Fuck.* He should've sprinted in at the beginning, but who was he to know that these lunatics would pick *now* to fire? Had they detected *Bluefish*? Or did his luck just suck?

Now wasn't the time to second guess himself.

"Conn, Sonar, torpedo hit! Big implosions bearing zero-four-two!" Walkman sounded as on-edge as everyone else. "Can't tell if she ate one torp or two, but that *Shang* is toast. Multiple implosions on that bearing."

"Conn, aye. What's the range to *Andromeda*?" Alex wondered if Revnik would show off her *Pictor's* top speed. Intelligence had a ton of contradictory estimates, but no real data. The *Pictors* were too new. Come to think of it, this was only the U.S. Navy's second close-in encounter with a *Pictor*...and likely the only one they'd get good data from. If war returned, *Bluefish's* data could be damned useful.

Assuming they survived today.

"Fifty-three thousand yards. She's inbound the boomer, speed six-four knots."

Alex whistled. "Damn, those *Pictors* must be sweet. You think we can get a tour?"

"I think an invitation for that would turn into an invitation to the gulag, Captain. Haven't you ever seen *Get Smart*?"

"The old one, the new one, or the bad one in the middle?" Alex grinned.

"Clearly not enough of them if you think asking to visit a Russian submarine is a good idea." Bobby shook his head, tsking like a cartoon character. "Unless you're looking for *really* cold retirement plan? You did go to school in the deep darkness of Vermont like a crazy person."

"I think I'll stick with Connecticut, thanks." The jokes helped lighten the atmosphere a notch, but it could never be enough. Not with the boomer's flooded missile tubes. Inaction itched. "Weps?"

Rose held up a finger, her eyes closed as she listened to the torpedo room via a headset. "Tube one reloaded! Tube two...ready! Reloaded!"

"Match bearings and shoot, tubes one and two!"

A few seconds passed, too many. Alex's heart rate wanted to go through the roof.

"Weapons away!"

"Conn, Sonar, two more fish running hot, straight, and normal."

"Conn, aye," Alex replied. "Weps, you know the drill. Do it again."

"Wires cut, outer doors closed." Rose never looked away from her console. "Reloading."

"Is it just me, or are the minutes going by in slow-mo?" Bobby asked in an undertone. "I feel like we're in some space-time screwup zone."

"Is that a technical term?" Alex asked.

"Yeah. Yes, sir, you bet it is."

Someone snickered, but again, it didn't last long. Alex swallowed. "Sonar, Conn, what's the boomer doing?"

"She's up to ten knots. No additional tubes flooded."

"You sure?"

"Sir, the sound of missile hatches opening is ingrained on my soul," Chief Andreas replied. "Best guess, two tubes flooded. Boomers generally do one port, one starboard to maintain stability."

"Captain, aye." Alex wished he could breathe right. His chest was so fucking tight that he felt like he might be having a heart attack.

Ten knots wasn't much speed, but it elongated the chase, both for *Bluefish* and her six torpedoes. At this rate, they'd get into Alex's preferred range in about a minute and a half, but reloading would take longer. *Andromeda* wasn't close enough to shoot, even though Revnik, too, was sprinting for all she was worth.

Except they might have an out. "COB, can a missile boat shoot at ten knots?"

"I wouldn't do it." Baker grimaced. "SLBMs are touchier than Harpoons, and we're *supposed* to slow to a maximum speed of five knots to shoot those out of vertical launch tubes. Preferably a hover."

"Wartime's proven a Harpoon can safely get out of the tube at ten knots." Alex didn't like the parallel, but he needed to know. He'd never served on a missile boat, and neither had any of his department heads. Master Chief Baker was the only one of his senior staff that had; thankfully, she was officer of the deck qualified—a rarity for enlisted sailors, even chiefs of the boat—and understood both the risks and the tactics behind the problem.

"You could try it, I guess," Baker replied. "Assuming you've got no qualms about dying if you screw up flooding those giant-ass tubes or having a missile that make it halfway out of the tube and then shit itself."

"That sounds pleasant," Bobby said. "Is it too much to hope that they actually *don't* have the launch codes?"

"From your lips to the ears of fate." Alex glanced at Liao. "Commander Fan?"

Liao pursed his lips. "Intelligence indicates that they likely received them from a communist defector."

"Fuck. There goes that idea." Alex glanced at his team. Chief Rhee remained laser focused on guiding the first torpedoes in. Two of Rose's other sailors monitored the other torps. The pair on the helm and lee helm looked calm, but their white knuckles told a different tale. The electronics and nav corner were quiet as those sailors worked, and the missile consoles were dark and silent.

His crew might well be the best in the world. If they couldn't pull this off, no one could.

"She's dropping noisemakers!" Walkman was back on the internal net, but Alex didn't get a chance to answer.

"Captain, ninety seconds to impact, torps one through four," Rose said.

Alex crossed to the sonar room and yanked the curtain aside. "Chief, if that boomer floods anything else—or you hear missile separation—I want you to scream bloody murder."

Chief Andreas kept her eyes closed and her head down, only throwing him a thumbs-up in response as she listened intently.

"On it, sir," Walkman said. She didn't look at him, either.

Nodding, Alex took the half-dozen steps that brought him back to the center of control. "What's our range?" he asked Bobby.

"Just under eleven thousand yards. Seven minutes until we're on top of her," Bobby replied. "If she speeds up more, she'll elongate the chase, but she's not fast enough to get away unless she grows wings. Or a giant alien whale comes along to give her a tow."

"The faster she goes, the less likely she is to get a shot off." Alex rubbed his aching forehead.

"In that case, you want me to give her a ring on Gertrude and encourage her to run faster?"

"Conn, Sonar, target speeding up. New speed fifteen."

"Run, you fucker," Alex whispered. "Run from those nasty little torpedoes like you have a damned chance."

Bobby snickered.

Alex's heart rate did not slow.

"*Bluefish's* torpedoes are in final acquisition," *Andromeda's* sonar officer reported.

"Very well." Katerina squared her shoulders. "Our range?"

"Still over thirty thousand yards, Captain. We are outside *Shkval* range."

Katerina did not let herself grimace. "Yes, I know, thank you."

For a moment, she contemplated reloading one tube with an older *Futlyar* but discarded the idea. Assuming *Bluefish* somehow missed—which would be hard, with six torpedoes in the water and the *Jin* being so obligingly slow—*Andromeda* would need every weapon at her disposal to sink them. Besides, the *Futlyars* might have a greater effective range than her super-cavitating *Shkvals*, but they still weren't what Katerina would call a long-range torpedo.

The new generation *Shkval* was in testing, she knew. The torpedo would only be a little faster than the −111 version, but it was planned to have much more range. Rumors said twice as much. But she hadn't been given a torpedo for testing—that job went to Dmitriy Kovalev, of course—so Katerina could not be certain. She shook herself. Those thoughts would not help her now.

"Are they firing?" she asked Daniil, who had served on a missile sub before *Andromeda*. Katerina's first boat had been one as well; however, Daniil had been a weapons officer. He knew more about this than she did.

"They can't fire from that speed. Our subs have interlocks to prevent it. I imagine the Chinese do, too, since they copied so much from us in the past," her second-in-command replied.

She steepled her fingers, sitting back in the small captain's chair in control. "So she will have to slow. Which will let the torpedoes catch up."

"*Da.* Likely. A *Jin* does not have the maximum speed to avoid any of those torpedoes. They'll top out around thirty-five knots, even if they sprint." Daniil chuckled. "And even American torpedoes are fast enough to catch a boat *that* slow."

"As we can see." Katerina grimaced. "Though must it take so long? I do not like waiting."

"Admiral Brovin will not be pleased that we let an American take the shot," Daniil said in an undertone. "We were meant to get in first."

Katerina sighed. "Alas, they were closer, and my priority is to save the world from nuclear devastation."

"You are also enjoying working with a submarine commander as competent as you. On your own level, so to speak."

"Yes, but we will not tell Admiral Brovin *that*." She finally chuckled, imagining her superiors' reactions to her cordial email exchanges with Alex Coleman. Not to mention calling him on the underwater telephone.

Her tactics were unorthodox, but it was the result that mattered.

Now if that damned *Jin* would just oblige them by eating a pair of torpedoes—one was not enough for lunatics who wanted to watch the world burn—everything would be all right. Katerina's naval career would survive and even thrive if the boomer went down. If not...

Regardless of what her superiors said, Katerina was not prepared to watch the world go up in flames just to deny an American victory. But she'd be ready. If Coleman and *Bluefish* failed, *Andromeda* would be ready.

Only nine thousand yards separated Alex's command from the Chinese boomer, but the Marianas Trench might as well have divided them. This rogue, bumbling enemy might not be professional submariners to match *Bluefish's* crew, but they'd still managed to draw this engagement out, squeezing out second after second.

"Thirty seconds until impact!" Chief Rhee's voice split the thick air of control, sending a new shiver down Alex's spine. "Torpedo one has reached the noisemaker...torpedo one off course! Torpedo two past the noisemaker. Three and Four still on the wire. Twenty-four seconds to impact for torpedoes two, three, and four."

"Conn, Sonar, missile separation!" Chief Andreas's voice was so loud Alex could hear it without the speaker. "Missile separation on the target!"

Bobby's head jerked up. "What the fuck?"

"They're throwing a Hail Mary." Alex grimaced. "Not surprising."

"They can't launch at that speed." Bobby turned to face Alex, his eyes like doorknobs. "Can they?"

"Without being on that sub, I'd say—"

"Conn, Sonar, almighty crash and bang, same bearing as the target." Now Walkman took over; Alex thought he could hear Andreas swearing in the background. "Now flooding."

Master Chief Baker beamed. "The idiots tried to launch at too high a speed. I think they got a fail-to-eject."

"And the missile fell back *down*?" Bobby's face went white.

"Sounds like," Baker replied, wearing a vicious grin.

It was a nice image, but Alex didn't have time to gloat. That boomer probably wouldn't sink from a failed missile ejection, and even if it did, the fucker could launch their *other* eleven JL-3 SLMBs. "Chief Rhee, time to impact?"

"Eight seconds." Rhee's voice was almost a whisper.

"Tubes one and two ready to launch!" Rose said.

Alex held up a hand. "Standby on the launch, Weps. Let's see how these three torps fare. There's already two behind them."

Those last two would be useless if any of the first three fish hit, and Alex could afford the handful of seconds with five active torpedoes chasing the boomer. A quick glance at the plot showed that *Andromeda* still had the pedal down; the Russian boat was racing to the fight as fast as she could. But they wouldn't arrive soon enough. These terrorists remained *Bluefish's* problem.

"Weps, aye."

"Five seconds."

"She's turning," Bobby whispered. "Coming left like she maybe wants to shoot back?"

"Better that than another missile," Alex replied.

No one moved. Despite his resolution to remain calm, Alex held his breath. Better that than telling his crew that they were riding in a ninety-two-hundred-ton weapon of their own. If all else failed, *Bluefish* had less than nine thousand yards—about six minutes—until she could straight-up smash that Chinese boomer.

How many missiles could they launch in six minutes?

"Three...two...torpedo two lost lock and circling! Torpedoes three and four—"

"Conn, Sonar, impact! Explosions bearing three-four-five! Multiple implosions. We got her, sir!"

Alex's knees went weak; he leaned against the periscope display as his body tried to turn into a limp rag. Thankfully, his brain kept working, and he cleared his throat. "Sonar, Conn, any further missile separation?"

"Negative, sir. Nothing turning and burning," Andreas replied. "I've got breakup noises on the target bearing."

"That's it? That's fucking it?" Alex asked no one in particular.

Bobby laughed and slapped him on the shoulder. "Congratulations, Captain, you just saved the world."

"*We* killed that sub, Bobby. There's no world in which this success doesn't belong to everyone on this boat."

Bobby beamed as Alex picked up the microphone for the 1MC. His crew had stepped up, just like they always did. They'd done the impossible. Now it was time to tell them just how much he appreciated that.

Chapter 10

Epilogue: Still-Burning Embers

28 May 2040, the South China Sea, IVO the Spratly Islands

Two hours after sinking *Changzheng 14*—and then telling the navy via official message that he'd done it—Alex's hands started to shake. Thankfully alone in his stateroom, he let himself bury his head in his hands for a few luxurious moments, relief flooding over him like an icy tidal wave.

"God damn," he whispered.

Thinking about what might have happened if *Changzheng 14* managed a successful missile launch was almost enough to make his mind fold under. Had the Chinese boat been diving a touch slower, or if they'd had a few more missile technicians on board... Alex shuddered. Thinking about the disaster it might have been left him cold. Millions could be dead now, or soon to be. Sure, someone might've shot the missile down, but if they hadn't, its launch would be all his fault.

The shrill ring of his stateroom phone made him jump. Sucking in a shuddering breath to collect himself, Alex grabbed the handset before it could screech for a third time. "Captain."

"Well, if it isn't the hero of the fucking hour." The accented voice made Alex's head whip around to eye the blinking light signaling *outside line call* on his phone. Shit.

"Admiral Rodriquez." Why would his goddamned hands not stop shaking? "Good to hear your voice, sir."

"You had me fooled there for a second, son. You sound like shit."

"It's been a long ten days." Alex let his eyes slide shut as exhaustion crowded in. "But I take it that you got our message. The job's done."

"And you're running shallow enough to take a call, which means you expected one." Marco Rodriquez didn't pull many punches, and he clearly wasn't starting today.

That was a pity, because Alex could use a fucking break. He sighed. "You're the third, sir. Got one from the squadron and one from Admiral Hamilton's office already."

"Well, fuck me silly. Here I thought I'd be the first."

"Sorry about your luck?"

Rodriquez laughed before Alex could curse his big mouth yet again. "Well, I'd sure as fuck prefer you to sink those would-be apocalyptic assholes and me be late off the mark to call you than *you* being late off the mark to sinking them."

"You and me both." Alex had a hard time keeping his voice above a half whisper. "It was a near thing, Admiral. They started launching while fleeing our torps, but their speed was too high and the missile crashed back down. Might've sunk them without the three hits, but I wasn't taking chances."

"Sounds more exciting than I'd like, that's for fucking sure," Rodriquez replied. "That VDR recording is probably going to be a classic."

Alex groaned. "Don't remind me."

"You've only got yourself to blame, Captain. You keep making history, we'll keep using it as a training tool."

Not swearing took all he had. Alex knew that the battle to save Convoy 57 had been turned into a simulation, but he wanted nothing to do with running that damn thing himself. He supposed their fight with Rochambeau would probably get the same treatment, and now this...

"You do realize how un-fucking-pleasant it is to be the 'tool,' right, sir?" So much for not swearing, but at least his audience wouldn't care, even if captains weren't supposed to swear at admirals.

"Better that than dead." Rodriquez didn't sound very sympathetic; Alex supposed such an outgoing character wouldn't understand his natural aversion to the spotlight.

"Yeah, that's true." Alex swallowed. "Can you avoid pinning a medal on me for this? I feel like not dying in a nuclear holocaust is reward enough. Besides, half the credit belongs to Captain Revnik and *Andromeda*, much though the navy won't like that."

There. He'd see what Rodriquez did with *that* trump card. Alex knew that—even in a shiny new world clinging to peace—cooperation with the Russians still wasn't the U.S. Navy's favorite flavor.

"You're maneuvering like fucking crazy to avoid a second Medal of Honor, aren't you?"

Alex's heart stopped. He knew enough history to know there hadn't been a dual Medal of Honor winner in something close to a hundred years, and he *sure* as fuck didn't want to break that trend. "Sir—"

"Cool your tits, Coleman. No one wants to create that precedent, even with this. If you *didn't* already have it, I'd slap one on you in a nanosecond, but I don't think we're ready for that. So count yourself lucky when I pin another Navy Cross on you."

"That is *not* what I'd call lucky." Alex wanted to scream, but if he objected too hard, would Rodriquez push for another Medal of Honor instead?

"Piss on your introversion. You'd bitch to high heaven if I didn't reward your crew appropriately, and *they'll* be put out if I fail to recognize you. This is one of those things you just have to live with as a leader."

Grinding his teeth would do nothing more than give him a headache; Alex relaxed his jaw with an effort. "Is this a shut up and color moment, then?"

"Yep."

"Aye, aye, sir." Saying more was pointless. They both knew Rodriquez had him over a barrel. Again.

"All right. Let's start talking about bringing you somewhere closer to home, shall we? The weather in Pearl is great this time of year."

Alex's eyebrows shot up. *Bluefish's* homeport had been Perth, Australia, since they shifted there at the war's start. But the war was over, or at least mostly over. As far as he knew, the armistice was still in place—hell, *Changzheng 14's* sinking hadn't even been officially announced yet—and that changed everything, didn't it?

"You really think peace will last?" he couldn't help asking.

"Fuck if I know, but we're going to give this thing a shot. You might've just done it, son. Let's get your boat out to Pearl so I can give a proper thank-you."

A few minutes later, Alex called up to control and had Rene work up a navigation plan for Pearl Harbor, Hawaii.

30 May 2040, the South China Sea, 100 nautical miles southeast of Singapore

STS2 Mary Zins glanced over her shoulder as Wilson approached the sonar corner in *Kansas's* control room. "We were all thinking of getting smashed when we get home," she said. "You want to come?"

Briefly, Wilson thought about his cracked resolve from a few days earlier. "Nah. I quit drinking. Used to make me into an epic-grade asshole."

"From what I hear, you were a creative asshole," she replied. "You think one night out would send you back to your crazy days?"

"Honestly, I'm not so keen on finding out." He was as limp as he'd ever been, though, and had been since learning his old boat sank that commanded-by-crazies boomer before it could light the world on fire. "Seems smarter."

"All right." Zins shrugged. "Your loss."

"Probably." Wilson chuckled, not saying that even a sober night on the town would probably be more fun for him than Commander Kennedy was having at the moment.

Had he needed to walk by the captain's stateroom on the way to control yesterday? Probably not, though a few guys *had* been doing switchboard maintenance on his usual route, forcing him to go around. While walking at the slowest pace he could manage, he heard the explosion of fury when Commander Kennedy found out that *Bluefish* had indeed gotten the bad guys...with help that wasn't his. Worse yet, it was *Russian* help. Not *Kansas*.

If Kennedy couldn't tell the world was at peace, that was his problem. But Wilson secretly enjoyed watching the captain not get his way. *He* made Wilson's forays into being a destructive asshole look A-plus innocent. Kennedy was trouble. Glory-hungry trouble who always got his way.

Fuck, if Wilson had a sea daddy like Kennedy did in Admiral Hamilton, he'd have made chief *long* ago. He might never have gotten busted down a rank. Certainly not twice. But Kennedy had so much top cover that he could twist his orders into a knot, just like he was doing now, lurking around at the bottom of the South China Sea instead of heading back to Perth. Was the man looking for trouble?

What a silly question.

Zins jerked back to face her console so fast that her neck crackled. Her hands flew up to pull both ears of her headset on, but by the time she had, Wilson had grabbed a spare and thrown himself down into the chair to her left.

"Officer of the Deck, passive contact! Passive contact bearing zero-two-one or two-zero-one!"

"Start a track," the officer of the deck replied.

"Datum dropped. Contact is intermittent," Zins replied. "Recommend maneuvering to resolve bearing ambiguities."

"Conn, aye," the OOD said. Wilson didn't hear him—it was Weps, not the captain's hated navigator—pick up the phone, but he knew standard protocol was to call the captain when an unknown contact was identified.

Meanwhile, Wilson let his hands race over the controls, isolating this sound and that as *Kansas* began to maneuver. The computer, whose library held the sonar signature of every known submarine class *and* individual submarine, couldn't make heads or tails of the sound, not at this range. But slowly, Wilson's trained ears and the computer chewed on the problem.

What clinched it for Wilson was that *he* didn't recognize the sound. Every class of submarine was a little different, and by knowing what to look for, a good sonar operator could hear blade count and auxiliary noises. Those were two of the top two indicators to listen to, and experience told him that while this one sounded Russian, he didn't recognize a specific class. The computer was supposed to go through the same process, just faster, but it still hadn't spit out a class when Wilson smacked himself in the forehead.

"OOD, I think we have a *Pictor* heading for the SOM," he said. "If the message we got from *Bluefish* is right, I'd say it's *Andromeda*."

"Why would they not be heading home?" Kennedy asked. "Russia through the Sea of Japan and the Sea of Okhotsk is faster. Not to mention smarter."

For once, Wilson couldn't argue with his captain. "No idea, sir. But I don't recall reports of any other *Pictors* being around here."

Kennedy growled out a sigh. "It probably is her. Damn armistice."

Yeah, Wilson didn't say, *peace sucks when you're out for glory*. Kennedy likely didn't care what the rest of his boat thought. Not him. He just wanted another shiny medal and didn't care whose blood he had to shed to get it. Wilson suppressed a snort. To be fair to the man, Kennedy was probably fine bleeding out a few liters of his own blood, provided it got him that sweet, sweet recognition.

"Your orders, Captain?" Oh, great. Song was there, too. She was Wilson's second favorite charmer.

Kennedy scowled. "Fuck it. We have to let her go. We're still at peace, remember?"

"That's a pity." Wilson turned in time to see Song's eyes narrow. "It would be nice to be the first boat to sink a *Pictor*."

"And I'd risk it if we could had a guarantee that the shooting would start again, but I saw that message about the president already selecting a special envoy to the U.N. for *peace*." Kennedy spat the last word like a curse.

"It won't last." Song shrugged. "But I suppose we must give it a chance."

Wilson wanted to scream at them, to smash their heads together until his captain and XO both admitted that peace was better for the world. Did they truly want glory so much that they'd let thousands or hundreds of thousands more die just for the sake of their *egos*? What the fuck was this world?

"Unfortunately," Kennedy said. "OOD, it's time to head south. Our orders say return to home port, so let the Russian go."

"OOD, aye," Weps said.

Wilson listened to *Andromeda* for another two hours, mostly to make sure that the computer was recording this track and his prestige-seeking captain couldn't double back and sink the poor bastards.

He was ninety-five percent sure Kennedy wouldn't start the war back up on his own initiative. However, judging from what the COB told him about Kennedy sinking a French destroyer before war was declared, there was no way to be sure. Could Wilson stop him? Probably not. But he didn't relax until Master Chief Casey came to control, met his eyes, and gave Wilson a firm nod.

Yeah, that was a man who knew what was what. Casey wasn't sure Kennedy would do the right thing, either, and they both sure as shit knew Song wouldn't stop him. So Wilson gave the COB a half smile and stayed another hour, even though he wasn't on watch. He sent Zins off to grab some dinner, however, swapping half the watch with her so he could babysit the insane officers. Zins didn't need to suffer with him. Rank had privileges, but sometimes the responsibilities just sucked.

Kennedy finally left control after *Andromeda* hit the edge of their sonar range, still muttering obscenities. Only then did Wilson let himself breathe again.

Andromeda sped through the South China Sea just a few knots over her best silent speed of thirty-two knots. Why? Katerina had not been given a reason in her first set of orders, only to head toward the Strait of Malacca. She didn't like leaving her boat naked like that, even in a new era of peace when people were supposed to wait to be fired upon before shooting. There were too many people like her who had learned to be quickest to shoot, who had taught *themselves* how to be deadly in this underwater game that the Russian Navy had abandoned in recent decades.

Two days after sinking the terrorists who labeled themselves the "Undersea Liberation Army," she had her answer and did not like it.

It was after dinner on *Andromeda's* clocks by the time the boat went to battle stations and she headed to control, her stomach full and purpose clear. Katerina understood what Admiral Brovin intended. She even knew it came from the highest command authority in Russia.

She just wasn't sure about how history would view *her* role in this escapade.

"You saw our orders?" she asked as Daniil came to stand beside her.

"*Da*. The crew is ready," her second-in-command replied.

"No comments?"

"I do not think there is anything to say." He shrugged. "We will do our duty and win glory for Mother Russia."

"Yes, we will." Katerina sighed. "Sonar, mark your track on the American aircraft carrier."

"Carrier bears two-zero-four, range eight thousand yards."

"Very well." Katerina eyed the carrier formation on her tactical plot, which was displayed on a giant viewscreen at the front of control. The carrier, *Forrestal*, was one the fifth newest in the American fleet, but she was also barely two years old. As far as Katerina knew, this was *Forrestal's* first foray into these waters...and it would also be her last.

As usual, an American carrier had a sturdy escort. In this case, it consisted of two cruisers flanking the carrier—sonar evaluation said both were *Bull Runs*—a frigate in the lead, and three destroyers bringing up the rear. Looking at those three made her lips twitch; why did the Americans have to bring one of each of their active classes to this engagement? This wasn't some grand fleet display.

"Their frigate will be best at anti-submarine warfare," Daniil said, his voice quiet. "Should we take her first?"

"The carrier first. Four torpedoes, I think. I have heard that those new *Valley Forges* need a great deal of killing." She did not mention that Rochambeau told her that. She did not need to like the man to understand his keen tactical mind. "Then two for each of the cruisers."

Even with VA-111 *Shkvals*, Katerina suspected she would not hit one of her three initial targets. The super-cavitating torpedo did not turn well. She cocked her head. Yes, the far cruiser, *Trenton* would probably escape. She did not mind overmuch. Katerina knew she would not sink this entire carrier group. Not with only ten tubes.

"And the last two torpedoes?" Daniil asked.

"Target the newest destroyer. The *Evans*-class," she said. Those destroyers were good sub hunters, not to mention more powerful than many nations' cruisers. That would be a good kill.

"Once we have fired, reload and target the frigate and the other destroyers," she said.

One of the *Pictor*-class's strengths was the ability to preload targets into the weapons computer. Those would auto-download to the torpedoes once loaded, cutting the time for calculating solutions down to the bone. No one would have accepted such a risk in peacetime, because a torpedo could wander off if its target was already on the bottom, but she was not looking at peace, was she?

No, Katerina's duty was to restart the war, thus denying America the chance to use their newfound prestige—courtesy of Alex Coleman sinking those ULA maniacs—to control the war-end negotiations. If they did so, Russia would be forced to give up much of the territory and stations she had gained in the Sea of Okhotsk, not to mention their new stations in the northern Pacific.

No, Russia could not allow that. Katerina might not like being the hatchet woman, but she was Russian to her core. She would do whatever her country needed...even if it meant becoming the poster girl for Russian aggression.

"Match bearings and fire," she ordered.

Twenty minutes later, when USS *Forrestal* (CVN 86) slipped beneath the waves, she was not alone. She was joined by all three destroyers, *Thomas Payne*, *Farley*, and *Daniel Iouye* and one of the two cruisers, *Okinawa*.

News reports later revealed a catastrophic loss of life. All seven ships of the carrier strike group had relaxed to peacetime steaming, and the majority of their watertight doors were open. *Okinawa* was the first to sink, followed by the destroyers and then the stubborn carrier. The frigate raced for *Andromeda's* position, however, and it was her helicopter launch that forced Katerina to clear datum and go evasive. That saved the frigate and the last cruiser, but Katerina did not mind.

After all, if shots were fired and no one survived, who was to know what happened?

This just wasn't how she intended to enter the history books.

Kansas was still in range, barely, but Wilson's practiced ear picked up the sound of explosions over eighty miles away. The sonar conditions were good enough that he could guess that *Andromeda* had fired, just not at who or why. Regardless,

Commander Kennedy made one of the more solid decisions of his career and sprinted for the "sound of the guns."

Kansas arrived just in time to see *Farley* (DDG 146) slip beneath the waves. Fuming and unable to find *Andromeda*, Kennedy shot a message off to COMSUBPAC so fast that their communications officer's fingers were probably smoking. Wilson busied himself with identifying which ships were still in action while Kennedy and Song discussed if they should join the recovery effort. Attack submarines didn't have much space to take on survivors, but there were at least a thousand men and women in the water—far too many for one surviving cruiser and frigate.

In the end, Kennedy being Kennedy, he surfaced the boat and pulled aboard anyone he could. Wilson didn't fool himself for a moment into thinking Kennedy's heart was in the right place, but *not* recovering survivors would make the captain look bad, so *Kansas* entered the rescue game as the sun set.

By the next morning, May 31st, 2040, the news reached America's East Coast and capital. The armistice ended almost as soon as it began. Ships and submarines rushed to return to the warzone, *Bluefish* included. Alex didn't wait; he turned his boat away from her track to Pearl Harbor and headed back to Perth, Australia. Orders to do so arrived shortly before midnight.

Then, by the first of June, World War III was back in all its glory.

END

Thank you so much for reading! Every reader means the world to Indie Authors like me—I absolutely could not do this without you! If you're looking for the next book available, continue on to *Rule the Waves* if you haven't read that yet. Or you can preorder *The Stars Shall Burn*!

If you aren't already a member of my newsletter, joining is free! You'll get a free short story from *War of the Submarine*, as well as a free fantasy novella. I also have other free stories, sneak peeks, and behind the scenes looks that I share with my newsletter readers, so if that interests you, sign on up!

I usually send newsletters once a month, twice max, so I promise I won't fill your inbox with spam. But you will get dibs on deals, news, and more. I even share dog pictures from time to time, because I have two crazy Siberian huskies who personify shenanigans.

Hit next if you're interested in learning more about how *Empty Quiver* was written—and why it published out of order in the series.

The Journey to Empty Quiver

If you've been with me for a while, particularly if you follow me on Facebook, you've heard that I like to write in order. But, I hear you asking, this book is numbered 5.5 and yet it came after book 6! What's up with that?

Yeah. That's a story.

First, I have to go back and tell you how *War of the Submarine* was born. Years ago, I started a story I called *Little Blue Ribbon*. This story grew and grew, getting *significantly* longer than anyone in their right mind wants to publish as a novel. But I finished it. And then I wrote what I thought was book 2, *Fortune Favors the Bold*. (More on that later).

Only then did I realize that the start of my "book 1," henceforth known as LBR, didn't address how the war began. Thus, *Cardinal Virtues* was born. Bam! All set, books 1-3 done, right?

Nope. Once I tried to line LBR with CV, I realized it didn't exactly...fit. So, I tore LBR apart, intending to split it and make two books. However, as I wrote more and more story, it became *three* books: *The War No One Wanted*, *Fire When Ready*, and *I Will Try*. Along the way, I wrote *Before the Storm* (prequel), *Pedal to the Medal* (which was originally part of WNW, but it just didn't fit), and *Clean Sweep*.

Am I a hot mess? Maybe. My original draft of LBR became three novels and a short story. But that brought me back to *Fortune Favors the Bold*.

Fun fact: the original outline for *Fortune Favors the Bold* actually contained the story through not only FFB (now book 5), but also through *Empty Quiver, Rule the Waves,* and the upcoming *The Stars Shall Burn*. Even worse, *Rule the Waves* and *The Stars Shall Burn* were originally one book, which was also intended to include the events of this novella, *Empty Quiver*. Confused yet?

I certainly was. Somewhere approaching the endgame of *Rule the Waves*, I realized that the book was *way* too long. So, it got split in half, and the events of *Empty Quiver* just didn't fit on the front end where they would've belonged. I wanted to get EQ out before RTW, but since I wrote almost two novels (SSB is 75% done), there just wasn't time.

Why add *Empty Quiver*?

So here we are. *Empty Quiver* does take place before *Rule the Waves*, and it fills in an important bit of in-universe history that will matter later. It was something I always wanted to write. While I'm portraying a non-nuclear World War III, I believe there would *have* to be a moment where the entire world gets slapped in the face by how bad it could be. This arc was always meant to be part of the narrative, and I'm particularly pleased that I can offer a novella staring Alex Coleman instead of a side character.

Why put Empty Quiver before Rule the Waves?

Short answer: my timeline between *Rule the Waves* and *The Stars Shall Burn* is very tight. In fact, the prologue for SSB takes place inside RTW! SSB picks up the day after RTW ends, and for a lot of reasons—including the fact that I'm 75% done with SSB—that would take an enormous amount of work to change. That would cause writing delays, and none of us really want that, do they?

Fun Facts from *Empty Quiver*

1. Katerina Revnik gets a lot of page time here. She's inspired by one of my favorite redeemable villains, Admiral Thomas Theisman, from the excellent *Honor Harrington* books by David Weber.

2. This book was originally titled *Ride the Storm*, a title I preserved for the final chapter.

3. Kennedy is really going to regret not sinking Revnik when he had the chance. I originally had him slated to *also* break the armistice, but as glory-hungry as he is, Kennedy's not that stupid. Kennedy is, however, based on one of *my* captains in the navy...as is his hatred for one of his department heads. I was fortunate enough not to be that person, but my heart still aches for the department head that our CO hated for no good reason.

4. I couldn't get Nancy Coleman or John Dalton into this

one, or it would've become a novel all by itself. I had a fun plot in mind where Nancy and *Cape St. George* almost get sunk by Dimitry Kovalev, but it just didn't fit. That may get recycled someday.

5. Speaking of *Cape St. George*, did you know that Nancy's cruiser is named after my first ship? Young Ensign Roberts was assigned to USS *Cape St. George* (CG 71) many years ago. I've still got great memories of that ship and my shipmates.

6. The title of chapter 4, "The World Turned Upside Down," is an obvious reference to the play *Hamilton*. It felt fitting as I wrote this around *Hamilton's* tenth anniversary.

Also by the Author

War of the Submarine

Before the Storm
Cardinal Virtues
The War No One Wanted
Fire When Ready
Clean Sweep
I Will Try
Fortune Favors the Bold
Empty Quiver
Rule the Waves
The Stars Shall Burn (coming soon)

War of the Submarine Shorts

Never Take a Recon Marine to a Casino Robbery (subscriber exclusive)
Pedal to the Medal

Age the Legacy

Shade
Shadow (Coming Soon!)
Night Rider
Before the Dawn (Coming Soon!)

Legacy Shorts

Prelude to Conquest (subscriber exclusive)
The First Ride (Exclusive on Ream)
City of Light (Exclusive on Ream)
Concordia (Exclusive on Ream)

Alternate History

Against the Wind
Caesar's Command

Other Works

Agent of Change (Portal Sci-Fi with an Alternate History Twist)
Fido (Exclusive to Ream)
Once Upon a Dragon (Fantasy Short Story)

About R.G. Roberts

R.G. Roberts is a veteran of the U.S. Navy, currently living in Connecticut and working as a Manufacturing Manager for a major medical device manufacturer. While an officer in the Navy, R.G. Roberts served on three ships, taught at the Surface Warfare Officer's School, and graduated from the U.S. Naval War College with a masters degree in Strategic Studies & National Security, with a concentration in leadership.

She is a multi-genre author, and has published in military thrillers, science fiction, epic fantasy, and alternate history. She rode horses until she joined the Navy (ships aren't very compatible with high-strung jumpers) and fenced (with swords!) in college. Add in the military experience and history degree, and you get A+ anatomy for a fantasy author. However, since she also enjoyed her time in the Navy and loves history, you'll find her in those genres as well.

You can find R.G. Roberts' website at www.rgrobertswriter.com. From there, you can join her newsletter! Joining the newsletter will get you a free novella or short story, set in either the War of the Submarine or Age of the Legacy universes (or both, if you like both genres). Newsletters are a once-a-month affair, so there won't be a ton of spam in your inbox, but you'll be the first to hear about sales, get sneak peeks of new writing, and get to read free short stories from time to time, too!

R.G. Roberts is also one of the authors trying the new story-centric site known as "Ream." It's like Pateron, but made for authors and readers – and especially for superfans! There you will have access to exclusive first looks at all of her works, including early access to chapters of novels, short stories, and more! You can find her Ream at www.reamstories.com/rgrobertswriter.

Printed in Dunstable, United Kingdom

77337401R00077